In Real Life

In Real Life

by
Clifford Fazzolari

Pittsburgh, PA

ISBN 1-56315-297-5

Paperback Fiction
© Copyright 2002 Clifford James Fazzolari
All rights reserved
First Printing—2002
Library of Congress #2001099553

Request for information should be addressed to:

SterlingHouse Publisher, Inc.
The Sterling Building
440 Friday Road
Pittsburgh, PA 15209
www.sterlinghousepublisher.com

Cover design: Jeffrey S. Butler - SterlingHouse Publisher
Book Designer: N. J. McBeth

Printed in The United States of America

8/7/02

TO Nancy,

Thank you for coming out — always make sure your real life is all you've imagined.

Cliff Faylin

Dedication

This book and every day of my Real Life is dedicated to my wife Kathy, and my boys Matt, Jake, and Sam.

Acknowledgement

My family and friends mean the world to me. I need to say thank you to the great friends that I've had throughout the years.

My parents, John and Lynda Fazzolari, made sure that I was prepared for everything this life could throw at me, and my brothers — John, Jim, and Jeff — inspired me every step of the way. And as life goes on, my family has grown larger — a special thanks to Dana, Lisa, Chuck, Lynn, and Mike. (You too, Andrea, Nicole, James, and Adam).

Of course, my in-laws have accepted me as one of their own. Thanks to: Mike & Lori, Jim & Carilee, and the only guy who likes Springsteen more than me — John. (And Briana, Ryan, Cory, Sara, Laura, Toni, Jennie, and Katie).

A special thanks to Carolyn and John Foutz for dealing with the boys on a daily basis and for your unwavering love and support.

And finally, to my two best supporters and the most wonderful sisters that a guy could ask for — to Corinne and Carrie Lynn — thank you — you're the best.

In Real Life

"The realist is the man, who having weighed all the visible factors in a given situation and having found that the odds are against him, decides that fighting is useless." — Raoul DeSales

Like millions of children growing up in the United States, I spent a lot of time watching television during my formative years. Of course, I was finally able to understand that television wasn't anything other than a lie meant to entertain me, I had already lost a step in the real world. I remember a lot of conversations in the early part of my life that started with, *"Yeah, but in real life..."*

Let me give you a few examples:

> "In real life, *The Six-Million Dollar Man* was married to the blonde on *Charlie's Angels*, and not *The Bionic Woman*."
> "In real life, spiderman isn't even a cartoon."
> "In real life, Rock Hudson likes men."
> "In real life, O.J. Simpson isn't a great guy."
> "In real life, Elvis is fat and isolated and it'll probably kill him."

Growing up, I had every one of the above-mentioned thoughts. Unfortunately, each realization came with a steady dose of regret. Why couldn't Lee Majors and Lindsay Wagner love each other? Why wasn't there a real Peter Parker who solved crimes by turning into a giant spider? Why wasn't Rock Hudson attracted to Doris Day? Why was O.J. smiling all the time if he was a bad guy? How could Elvis be so cool one minute and so out-of-whack the next?

It's because that's what life is about. Reality is distorted by the lies we tell to get through the day. In the end, on our deathbeds, there will be a revelation of sorts. We'll simply close our eyes and slip off to the great beyond, realizing that we were gullible about everything. The ultimate smack of reality will be when St. Peter meets us at the main gate and reveals it's all been one big joke.

This is the story of a man who went through life believing that Santa Claus was coming down the chimney with a bag filled with presents.

Chapter 1

– Santa Claus is Dead – December, 1979

"I never believed in Santa Claus because I knew no white dude would come into my neighborhood after dark."
— *Dick Gregory*

I was only six years old. It was the night before Christmas 1979, and the house was deathly quiet except for the sound of my older brother, Michael, snoring in the bed across the room. I remembered our conversation from earlier in the day. We had discussed the fact that Santa Claus might be something of a made-up notion.

"If you think about it," Michael had said, "it's all pretty strange. What does Santa do when there isn't a chimney?"

I shrugged my shoulders. I was caught up in the excitement of Christmas, but Michael was threatening to take it all away.

"Does he break a window?" Michael asked.

"Maybe the parents of those kids leave the doors open," I suggested.

Michael contemplated this for a moment, but I knew he didn't believe in Santa anymore.

"What about the cookies? He can't possibly eat a cookie at every house," Michael said. "He's fat, but a cookie at every house?"

Now, my mind was reeling with the fight between reality and fiction. The night was unbelievably quiet. Michael was breathing heavy, and for the first time in my life, I was actually scared that things weren't what they seemed. My mind returned to our previous conversation.

"Then there's Rudolph," Michael said. "Does he really have a shining red light for a nose? Is it a bulb that needs changing?"

"I don't know," I shrugged. "It could be true."

"Think about it," Michael said. "He's a freak. No wonder the other reindeer laugh at him."

I went to my father with the new information. I explained what Michael said, and Dad laughed.

"Of course, Santa Claus is real. Who else would bring you presents?"

Lying in bed, I formulated my plan. I would, once and for all, prove the existence of the big red man. I knew that what I was about to do was wrong, but I couldn't help it. I had to find out for myself.

I heard what clearly sounded like feet on the roof. I knew that the reindeer would land quietly, but I'd seen enough pictures of Santa to realize that when he set all his weight down, I'd be able to hear the shingles creak.

I sat up in bed, expecting to see clear to the hallway, but darkness covered me. I took a deep gulp of air and held it in. My brother snored and turned in bed and I waited until I heard another noise from outside before moving. The wind howled and I imagined the big man preparing for his slide down the chimney.

I carefully moved to the side window. It was Buffalo, New York at the end of December and the snow was flying. *Santa will definitely need Rudolph tonight*, I thought, and I almost laughed.

I saw a red light in the distance and my heart jumped, but as much as I wanted to believe, the light was only a passing car. I slid the window open a crack and pushed the snow-covered screen to the ground. It was just a short drop, but I wasn't prepared for the coldness that grabbed hold of my tender bones. Still, I dropped to the ground and pulled the window down behind me.

I waited outside for what seemed like an eternity. I had no way of knowing whether Michael had heard me. The only thought in my head was that I was glad my mother had put me into the pajamas with the feet.

I looked to the roof. It appeared all was quiet, but I had no way of being sure until I could see the very top of the house. I pedaled backwards towards the street, staring at the rooftop. There was no red light shining from Rudolph's nose. I did not see a grotesquely fat man struggling to jam

2

his way into our chimney. In fact, the roof looked exactly as it had every day of my short life.

It was getting cold. Still, I waited. I glanced up and down the quiet street, wondering if Santa was caught up at one of the neighbor's houses. I couldn't imagine that he'd stop at Aaron's house. If it was true that Santa was watching us all the time, that kid didn't have a prayer. Aaron was a living terror who drove his parents to the absolute brink of insanity. I knew for a fact that Aaron had busted the side window of his father's car with an ice ball. The kid ate boogers, for crying out loud. There was no way that Santa would bring him presents.

The wind howled and a gust of snow flew directly into my face. I brushed the snow away and coughed. My feet hurt and my hands felt like they were about to fall off. I took a couple of steps, hoping that the movement would bring me some warmth. What if Santa wasn't planning to stop at my house this year? God only knew that my parents had threatened me enough times in the last few weeks. *Eat all your dinner or Santa won't come. Go straight to sleep or Santa Claus will bring you coal. Don't talk back to me. Do you think Santa likes boys who talk back?*

The moon was shining brightly above our house. There was a steady stream of smoke billowing from our roof. Maybe it was the quiet air or perhaps my brain had frozen, but it suddenly dawned on me. Santa Claus was a big fat hoax. There wasn't any Rudolph. There weren't any elves. Santa was a bribe, and the Easter bunny and tooth fairy probably were, too. Why had Mom and Dad pulled such a scam on us? My mother and father were lying to me. How could they do such a thing, and in good conscience ask me to go straight to sleep? How could I not talk back after realizing what a sham all of this was?

But suddenly, I heard a noise. I looked to the roof and to the spot where Santa would probably land the sled. There wasn't anything there. I heard someone calling my name and a wave of panic swept through my veins.

"Leo?" the voice called out. "What are you doing?"

I was sure that if I turned around Santa would be right behind me. A feeling of dread filled my little body as I realized that I had blown it. Santa would want to know why I was out of bed in the middle of the night. He'd want to know how I expected to get even a single present after pulling such a stunt.

3

"Hey, you idiot, what're you doing?"

If it was Santa calling out to me, I could handle it, but he wasn't going to get away with calling me names. I searched the night for a sign of him, glancing up and down the street.

"You're so stupid," the voice cried out. "You're going to freeze."

"Where are you, Santa?" I called.

I wanted to cry. Santa was calling me an idiot.

"I'm up here," the voice said. It sounded as if he were laughing.

For the first time, it occurred to me that Santa sounded an awful lot like Michael.

"I'm going to get Dad," he said.

I fell onto my back in the snow beneath my bedroom window. I looked up at Michael with tears welling in my eyes. *Why was everyone lying to me?*

It was only the start of what was to come.

◊ ◊ ◊

That Christmas Eve night will go down in infamy. My father sat Michael and I down at the kitchen table and waited for my mother to join us. Dad just sat there, with his glasses hanging on the edge of his nose and a look of fatigue in his eyes. Every once in awhile, he'd look at me and snicker. I was scared, angry and frightened all at once. Michael, despite the fact that he'd never left his bed, was crying as though we were about to be whipped.

My mother stepped into the room, coughing and retching as she reached for a cigarette. I looked at the clock, noting that it was just a little before one. I had never actually seen the kitchen clock at one in the morning.

"So you were looking for Santa, huh?" Mom asked. She had a pair of pajamas with her and she tossed them to me. My feet were aching from the cold, but I was afraid to mention it. I grabbed the pajamas, stepped out of the blanket my father had thrown at me, and waited for the anger to take control.

"Maybe now's the time to tell you," Mom said. She drew on the cigarette and coughed lightly. She looked at my father and he nodded.

"Santa Claus isn't real," she said. "Dad heard you guys talking today, and we figured that it'd be better if you heard it from us."

I couldn't help the tears. I glanced at Michael, and even though he was no longer crying, he looked a bit stunned.

"Who buys the presents?" Michael asked.

"We do," Dad said.

I looked at Michael as if to say Dad was lying again.

"You dress up in a red suit and come down the chimney?" Michael asked.

Mom and Dad laughed. They shook their heads as though we were just plain dumb.

"It's not funny," I said. "Why would you lie about something like Santa Claus and Rudolph?"

My father drummed his fingers on the kitchen table. He held out his arms for me and I stepped into them. I couldn't stop the tears from falling. Being held by Dad wasn't an every day occurrence, and it tore at my heart. The words that fell from my father's lips would stay with me for the rest of my life.

"This is a new stage in your life," he said. "At every turn, you'll look back and wonder why you believed the things you believed. I'm forty-one and I wonder how I could've been so stupid to believe what I believed at thirty-one."

I wasn't real sure what he meant, but Santa Claus was dead and it was only my first painful realization. In time, I would come to know exactly what my father was trying to tell me.

Chapter Two

– What really happens when you pull daddy's finger? –
December, 1981

"I phoned my dad to tell him I had stopped smoking.
He called me a quitter."
— Steven Pearl.

In 1968, Sara Ann Hundley met David Brown at a small-time construction company on the outskirts of Buffalo, New York. He was a carpenter foreman and she was the receptionist. It should've been the stuff of dreams. They should have raised Michael and I, and lived happily ever after into old age.

Such a scenario could not possibly be mistaken for real life.

I don't remember all the lurid details, but at eight years old, I was able to take in enough information to understand that something was brutally wrong with life around my house. In fact, in every life there are moments that clearly define who we are and what we become. When such a moment is before you at the age of eight, the true meaning of it can escape you.

It was late one night when my father stumbled through the door.

"Where were you?" Mom screamed.

"It's none of your business," he answered.

His words sounded funny to my young ears.

"You're drunk! You were with her, weren't you?"

Mom was crying. Dad was mumbling something about it being over.

"This isn't a marriage," he said. "It's a damn witch hunt."

Yet, whenever I asked either Mom or Dad about it, they told me that I couldn't possibly understand. So, I did what any other little boy would do - I played with my friends.

My best friend, Steve Anderson, was always at my house. He lived with his mother in a small trailer at the end of our road. Steve was always dirty, his clothes were usually torn, and he didn't ever have to be home at any special time. In children-speak, he had it made. No one ever yelled at him for being bad and sometimes I wondered what he ate for dinner. Steve didn't have to go to church, he wrote on the walls of his home with crayons, he never had to pick up his room, and I knew for a fact that he got to stay up way past nine o'clock. Yet, what I envied most about him was that Claire Bennett was in love with him. Even at such a young age, the haves and the have-nots are clearly distinguished. Steve had what it took to get girls to like him and I didn't.

Steve, Claire, Michael and I spent a lot of our early days together. My mother called us the four musketeers and my father said we were the rat pack. I didn't know what any of it meant, but I hated school because I missed hanging out with my special friends. I can't say I knew all that much about what distinguished a girl from a boy, but I felt really strange when Claire hung around with Steven. Mom and Dad were having even bigger problems. I'm not sure when the fighting started. I wasn't certain why my father spent more time at work than he did at home. The thing is, I missed him. The fact that he wasn't home all that much propelled me into a fantasy world of sorts.

My single, most important fantasy involved the Buffalo Sabres. In 1980, the Sabres were in first place and the news stations were filled with talk of the Stanley Cup. Championship-type hockey was something that Buffalo wasn't really familiar with, but I was certain that my beloved Sabres would win it all. The Sabres had three big stars back in the days of my youth: Rene Robert, Richard Martin, and Gilbert Perreault, yet, in my mind there was a fourth huge star in Buffalo. One day, without reason, and in front of my entire class and my teacher, Mrs. Jenson, I explained that my father had played professional hockey with Richard Martin, but had to quit because he had a bad knee.

"Leo, is that true?" Mrs. Jenson asked.

7

A couple of kids snickered, but I kept my eyes on the object of my affection. Claire Bennett never batted an eyelash.

"It's *true*," I said, "he scored fifty-six goals once."

As far as I knew, my father couldn't even stand up on skates. It was Steven Anderson who tried to expose me.

"Where'd he score fifty-six goals," he asked, "in your backyard?"

This time, the entire class laughed at me. I was in too deep.

"You laugh," I said. "Richard Martin was at my house three weeks ago."

It evolved into a typical argument between two kids.

"Richard Martin doesn't know your father," Steven said.

"Does too."

"Does not."

Mrs. Jenson ended it. "Leo, why don't you come out into the hall with me?" she asked.

Going out into the hall with Mrs. Jenson was the absolute worse possible punishment. I did what I could — I started to cry. I shot a look of pure hatred at Steven, but I didn't dare look at Claire.

"Hey, if you see Gordie Howe out there, tell him we said hello," someone yelled from the back of the room. Everyone laughed and I felt like sliding under the door.

◊ ◊ ◊

Mrs. Jenson, bless her heart, wasn't quite so cruel. She made me admit that it was a big fat lie, and there was a tremendous look of despair in her eyes when she asked me why I'd make up something about my father.

"My Mom hates him," I said.

"That's not true," Mrs. Jenson, said. "I know your Mom and Dad."

"She does," I said. "I'm not lying."

Mrs. Jenson bent to one knee. She held my face in her hands and wiped away a couple of tears. I was eight years old and I was crying in front of my teacher. It was the most humiliating thing that could happen to a guy.

"What would make you say something like that?" she asked.

"She caught him kissing another girl," I said. "Then, last night, Dad wouldn't even sit with us for dinner. He sat in the living room, drinking beer, and every time Mom said something, he yelled at her."

Mrs. Jenson pulled me close and I sobbed on her shoulder. It was a lesson that I had to learn. My Dad wasn't a professional hockey player. He didn't do anything special in life and at that moment, I knew he wasn't even a very good guy.

"Maybe we'll go talk to your Mom and Dad together," Mrs. Jenson said.

"I tried to talk to Dad last night," I said.

I leaned away from her, totally embarrassed by my crying.

"What happened?" Mrs. Jenson asked.

"He told me to mind my own business, and then he called me over and told me to pull his finger. I thought it was magic."

Mrs. Jenson held a look of pity in her dark brown eyes.

"You know what happened?" I asked.

"Yes," Mrs. Jenson said, "I think I do."

"Why would he do that?" I asked.

"I don't know," Mrs. Jenson said. "Sometimes we expect something different from grown-ups, don't we?"

I guess I was beginning to understand a little because I buried my head in Mrs. Jenson's shoulder one more time.

◊ ◊ ◊

Suddenly, the fighting stopped. The house became too quiet. Mom and Dad just seemed to stop talking to each other. I don't know about Michael, but I was afraid to even make a sound. The absolute silence was even worse than the screaming.

To my parents' everlasting credit, they didn't make us suffer. Yet, I'm not sure what either of them was thinking when they loaded us into the car and drove out into the country.

"We have a little surprise for you," my father said. "You boys are going to really like it."

Given the fact that they were sitting beside each other after weeks of screaming, there wasn't too much we would have found disappointing.

"Things are going to be a little different when we get home," Mom said.

She was speaking real soft and slow and I knew something was up.

"You know how it is when Dad goes away on business," she said.

"It's just the three of us," Michael said.

9

"Exactly; that's how it'll be for awhile," Mom said.

I looked at my ally in all of this and Michael shrugged his shoulders like he couldn't care less. I dropped my eyes away from Mom's demanding glare. She wanted some sort of reaction and I wouldn't give her the satisfaction. Steven's father was never home and they lived like pigs. I didn't want that to happen to us.

"I'm going to be living a little ways away," Dad said.

I wanted to reach over the seat and slap the back of his head. This was entirely his fault. It took all my strength to blink back the tears.

"You're getting a divorce, right?" Michael asked.

It was Mom's turn to drop her eyes.

"We just need some time apart," my father said.

"So you'll come home again in a little while?" Michael asked.

We both knew there wasn't any sense in getting excited.

"I'll be around all the time," my father lied.

He angled the car down a long, winding driveway. There was a barn and some horses off in the distance and I concentrated on the sight of the animals, but the tears clouded my vision.

◊ ◊ ◊

The reason for the ride into the country was a small, white dog with huge black spots, or was it a small black dog with huge white spots? Archie was a little ball of fire. He jumped into my lap and licked my face. Michael joined in the fracas and Mom and Dad stood off to the side admiring us as if we were still a family. Even at such a young age, I remember thinking that I would grow to hate Archie because he was to be my father's replacement.

On the way home, Archie jumped from lap to lap. I couldn't wait to show him off to Claire and Steven.

"There's only one thing wrong with him," Mom said.

It was as if the other shoe had finally dropped. She would tell me that Archie had cancer and wouldn't live a week; or worse yet, it was all a lie and we'd have to take him back in the morning.

"Look at his tongue," Mom said. "It doesn't fit all the way back into his mouth."

It was almost impossible to detect as Archie hardly ever settled down, but at one point he sat between Michael and I and tried to close his mouth. There was about an inch of his tongue sticking out and within seconds it grew dry. Archie took it all in stride and it was about the coolest thing I had ever seen. I hugged the dog to my chest and the image of my mother's smile burned into my mind. I knew she wouldn't be smiling much anymore.

◊ ◊ ◊

Archie was a tremendous hit. Claire sat in the center of the kitchen hugging and kissing Archie as though they'd been together all their lives. As ridiculous as it sounds, the sight of Claire kissing anything made me jealous. In the background, my father and his friends were removing items from our house. As the novelty of Archie began to run thin, I took to watching my father's exodus.

"We're going to play hockey at the park," Steven announced in the middle of it all.

"That sounds like a nice idea," Mom said, no doubt noticing what I was watching.

Claire rubbed Archie's belly and Archie kicked his left leg out as if he were scratching himself.

"I'll play," Michael said.

"How about you?" Steven asked me.

They both knew my answer. I would only play if Claire was playing and we were on the same team. We all looked in her direction.

"I'll play if Archie can come with us," Claire said.

Four heads turned in Mom's direction. She had tears in her eyes and I knew she wanted us out of the house. At that moment, she probably would've agreed to a plot to assassinate the mayor of Buffalo.

"I suppose," she said. "I have a collar and leash. Leo's in charge of walking him."

It was as if everything was now miraculously right in my life. I hugged my mother.

"He'll have fun, but he'll probably chase the puck," she said.

11

We didn't care. I brushed by my father on the way out of the house and he grabbed me to his chest and squeezed me so hard that I thought he'd break a rib. I think he said he loved me, but it didn't matter. I had Archie, Claire and hockey. Who needed him?

I played my heart out. There were ten people there and the game was tied four to four. Claire had scored all of our goals and we had hugged after each one. Archie was waiting patiently for us on the sidelines and as the puck was placed at center court for the face-off to decide the game I lapsed into a daydream.

> *I was racing down the wing at Memorial Auditorium. Rene Robert passed me the puck just as I got in front of the Flyers' goalie, Bernie Parent. I lifted the shot up over his shoulder seconds after he dropped to make the save. The crowd went wild and I raised my stick high above my head and scanned the crowd for Mom and Dad, but their seats were empty.*

"Hey, stupid, you ready?" Claire was inches from my face. "We've got to win this."

I looked right through her to the sidelines.

"Where's Archie?" I asked.

Claire's head spun around as if she were possessed by something and moments later, we were running down the street in different directions in search of Archie.

◊ ◊ ◊

We met back at the park about twenty minutes later. There wasn't a dry eye around and I was crying harder than anyone. Mom had put me in charge of watching Archie and I had lost him on the very first day.

"We'll split up," Steven said. "I'll go with Claire back towards your house and you guys can look in the woods back there."

"I think Leo should go with Claire," Michael said. "She knows how to calm him."

We walked in silence for the first few minutes, and Claire slipped her arm around my right shoulder.

"It'll be all right," she said. "Dogs know a lot about making it on the streets."

12

"But he never lived around here," I said. "What if he gets lost?"

"We'll find him," Claire said.

My father used to tease me about liking Claire. He used to make kissing sounds and say that we'd be married someday. At first it bothered me, but then it didn't matter. I wanted to marry Claire. I liked her golden hair and blue eyes. I liked the way she was always laughing and telling me it would be all right. I liked when she put her arm around my shoulder, and she was the best hockey player I knew.

"There he is!" Claire broke away from me and started running down the middle of the road. Archie was off to the left shoulder, but he heard the sound of Claire's voice and turned to her. We were no more than seventy-five feet away when the car barreled into Archie. His little body soared high into the air and the squealing brakes made a deafening sound. I kept running, but I knew that I didn't want to get there.

Claire bent down over Archie's lifeless body. She pulled his bleeding snout towards her. The tip of Archie's tongue was hanging from his mouth. Claire was wailing so loudly that I covered my ears with my hands. A man, about the same age as my father, swung his car door open. He extended his arms wide as if none of it were his fault.

"I never saw him," he said.

"Is he dead?" I asked.

"I'm sorry, son," the man said.

Everyone was always so sorry, but my Dad was gone, Archie was gone and Claire was rocking the dog back and forth as blood splattered the front of her shirt.

"My mother says when it's time to go to God, we have to go," Claire said. "My grandmother went to God and now Archie's going. You have to go when you're called."

She had blood all over the front of her Sabres jersey. I kept looking at Archie's face and the tip of his tongue. In the strangest of all things, he looked almost peaceful, but why did God have to call Archie today?

Chapter Three

– Little League only lasts four years – April, 1984

"Show me a hero and I'll write you a tragedy"—F.Scott Fitzgerald

My father moved into a tiny apartment three streets away. In the years immediately following the divorce, Michael and I made the trek to visit Dad as though he were our favorite uncle. Dad became sort of a solid fixture in our lives, but his girlfriend Margaret did, too, and I don't know about Michael, but I could've lived without her.

In those days, my father and I could not get close to one another. I considered the divorce to be my father's fault and he held that against me. He considered me to be something of a weakling and I held that against him.

One day in late April of 1984, the subject of little league baseball came up. The dinner lineup in those days was always the same. Michael sat on my father's right side, and my seat was as far away from him as their dining room table would allow. Of course, that put me on Margaret's right, so I had to take the good with the bad.

"So, baseball starts next week, huh?" Margaret asked.

She was always smiling and it drove me absolutely crazy. She was nice just so we'd choose her over our mother and it was maddening.

"I can't wait," Michael said.

Michael was the Mets' hard-hitting third-baseman. Each and every year, he made the all-star team.

"We're going to win it all this year," Michael continued. "We have Claire at short, and Steven at first. All we need is a decent second-baseman, and we'll have the best infield in the league."

All eyes turned to me. I was staring down at my mashed potatoes, wishing that I could bury myself inside. Up to that point, little league baseball was a living hell.

"What about Leo?" Margaret asked. "He can play second."

Michael snickered, and I looked up just in time to see Dad enjoying a knowing smile.

"We have to get Leo to take some ground balls," Dad said.

The reality of it all was that I just plain sucked. I ran the details of the two previous seasons through my mind. Every night I would grab my glove and head off to practice, and on game days, I would sit at the end of the bench and wait until the score got well out of hand so I could stroll up to the plate and strike out on three pitches. Mom was always at the games and I would watch her cheering for Michael. It broke my heart that she was so pitifully enthusiastic when I came to bat. One night it was so bad that she actually bought me an ice cream cone for fouling off a pitch. I guess she thought it was a grand gesture, but I cried myself to sleep that night.

"You know, I've got an idea," Dad said. "What if I coach the team?"

It was the absolute worst idea I'd ever heard.

"Al Stevens is our coach," I said. "We all like him."

"He's a nice guy, but you'll never win it all with him coaching. Your old man could make sure you win the championship."

Michael was absolutely beaming. Dad leaned back in his chair and considered the idea.

"I'd be able to see you guys a lot," he said. "We'd get a lot closer, and Leo, you'd be able to play all the time."

It didn't make sense to me. He had cheated on our entire family and now he wanted to coach our team to get closer to us? If he had stayed home where he belonged, he probably wouldn't even consider the notion.

"I think I'm going to do it," he said.

He was waiting for me to smile, but I just couldn't do it. Actually, I was considering suicide.

◊ ◊ ◊

It only got worse for me. On the first day of practice, my father anointed me the new leadoff hitter and starting second baseman. I *nearly*

15

screamed when he made the announcement, and the rest of the team *actually* did.

The Yankees were the best team in the league in those days and most of it was because they had a man-child by the name of David Bryant. David was the meanest kid in class. He was already six-feet tall and one hundred and sixty pounds, and he threw the ball so hard that there wasn't a kid in the league who wanted to bat against him. David was especially nasty to me in those days because he had a slight crush on Claire and I was one of Claire's best friends.

On the night before the first game of the season, Claire, Michael, Steven and I were walking home after practice. When Steven and Michael were out of earshot, I confessed my fears to Claire.

"I can't go up there against Bryant," I said.

"You're our first hitter," Claire said. "Just watch the ball from the moment it leaves his hand and be ready to swing."

"He's going to drill me," I said.

"No, he won't. You can't think about it," Claire said. "Besides, you've been hit before — it won't hurt that bad."

"It won't hurt you," I said.

All at once, an idea struck me.

"He's in love with you," I said.

"Who? David?" Claire acted as if she didn't know that we all secretly loved her.

"I was thinking you could tell him not to hit me."

I offered my best puppy dog eyes and Claire considered it for a moment.

"I'm sorry," she said, "I can't do that. You have to learn to stand on your own on this one."

Claire slipped her arm around my shoulder and gave me a hug that a sister might give.

"I think you're going to get a big hit off of him," she said.

◊ ◊ ◊

Before the game started, I stood off to one side of the field playing catch with Claire. It didn't matter that I missed most of the balls that she threw at me, or that the ones that I caught hurt my hand. She was always my partner.

"What you have to do is get into a little crouch," she said. "Keep a good eye on the ball. David's a big guy, but he'll walk you every time if you watch the ball."

I couldn't even describe the nervousness I felt. Mom sat in the first row of bleachers with Dad's girlfriend directly behind her. I know Mom hated Margaret, but there wasn't much I could do about it. I had my own problems.

I saw Bryant warming up on the Yankees side of the field. He looked at me and laughed. I thought about picking up a bat, walking over to him and slapping that grin off his face. Chances are, I would've swung and missed.

My father called us together before the start of the game and we got into a huge circle.

"Okay," Dad said, "everyone knows the Yankees are the best team in the league, but this year we're going to be the champs, right?"

We all yelled "Right!"

We joined hands and on the count of three, we all screamed out "Mets!" My father read the lineup and I couldn't believe he was going through with it.

"Batting first and playing second base is Leo Brown," Dad said.

The hot dogs I'd eaten before the game threatened to show as I picked up my favorite bat.

"Come on, Leo!"

"Show him where you live, Leo!"

My knees were shaking. The ump cried out to play ball. I took a couple of very deep breaths and strolled towards the batter's box. Bryant watched my every move and I saw his eyes grow mean when Claire ambled to my side to wish me luck. She leaned to my ear and whispered, "Come on, buddy, stand up for yourself."

I stepped into the batter's box and tapped the dirt off my spikes. I touched the far corner of the plate and the ump asked me if I was ready. I nodded and took a couple practice swings.

Bryant stared me down. His cap was pulled down on his forehead and he actually grinned. My knees shook so bad that I prayed I wouldn't fall down before the first pitch. Bryant reared back and fired and the ball got bigger in a split-second. It came straight for the middle of my forehead and I hit the deck just in time. The ump screamed that it was a ball and my bench congratulated me for my good eye.

The second pitch came out of Bryant's gigantic hand at an even quicker pace. Once again, it was directed at my right temple. As I hit the ground, two things fought for space inside my head. First off, Bryant was laughing at me, and secondly, I had urinated in my pants. It wasn't that I had soaked the entire uniform, but there definitely had been a release.

Out of the corner of my eye, I saw Claire warming up in the on-deck circle. No matter what was about to happen, I couldn't let her know that I had pissed myself. I glanced down at the front of my pants and to my horror I met the catcher's eye. He started to laugh, but neither one of us had time to think. The third pitch came straight down the middle and I let it pass.

"Wait for your pitch," Dad screamed.

"You pissed yourself," the catcher said.

I dropped my hand over my cup and stepped back into the box. I just wanted it over before the catcher could announce to everyone I ever met that Leo Brown, at the ripe old age of eleven, had wet his pants out of sheer panic.

The next pitch headed for my chin and something held me right there. The ball crashed into the side of my helmet and the world faded to black for a second. I swear I heard David Bryant laughing as the rest of the urine made its appearance. As I lay sprawled on the ground with warm urine soaking me from waist to knee, I had the presence of mind to turn onto my stomach. I didn't care if I had a massive concussion, I just couldn't live with the rest of it.

Claire was the first person to reach me.

"Leo, are you all right?" she whispered.

She was the last person that I wanted to know, but the only one who could save me now.

"I peed my pants," I whispered. "You have to get me out of here without anyone seeing me."

All eyes were on Claire and me. My mother was squealing; my father was telling me to get down to first; the umpire was waiting to see if I was dead or alive and the catcher was laughing uproariously.

"What should I do?" I whispered.

"Get up and run into the woods," Claire whispered.

She backed everyone away from me as though I were suddenly contagious. I heard her tell the catcher that she'd kill him if he ever mentioned anything to anyone.

I jumped up and ran away with my hands firmly clasped over my cup.

◊ ◊ ◊

The night gathered around me. I can't ever remember crying as hard as I did that night. I was ashamed of myself for failing and I was angry with Dad for putting me into such a position. As much as I loved baseball and as much as I wanted to be a big part of the team, the reality of it all was that I wasn't anything more than a walking catastrophe.

I was perched in a huge oak tree in Claire's backyard. My mother was probably going out of her head with worry, but this was bigger than her. I couldn't run to her on this one. Claire would find me and talk me out of the tree, but as far as I was concerned, the rest of the world could just go to hell.

I heard Claire's voice and I knew that she would come for me alone. She directed Michael and Steven to look for me back at my house and moments later, I heard her at the base of the tree.

"Can I come up?" she asked.

"I don't know why you'd want to," I said.

Claire was like a little monkey. She climbed the tree in seconds and I moved to one side so she'd have space on my branch.

"We won," she said.

I really didn't have a suitable response to that bit of news.

"Bryant put on a real show. The umpire threw him out of the game."

I half-chuckled, but I was too ashamed to look Claire in the eyes. She placed her hand on my right knee.

"Why do you even bother talking to me? I'm the biggest loser in town."

"You know you're not," Claire said. She looked to the front of my pants where the pee had dried.

"Everyone's going to find out," I said.

19

Claire took a deep breath. She put her arm around my shoulder and gave me a quick squeeze.

"No one will find out," she said. "No one said anything. Everyone was worried about you."

"I wish that pitch would've killed me," I said.

When Claire spoke again it was evident that she was losing her patience. She would put up with all of my crap, but she hated when I started feeling sorry for myself.

"You want to die because you peed your pants?" she asked. "Do you think there's a person out there who hasn't pissed themselves? Do you think any of us have it easy?"

I wasn't sure what she was getting at, but I knew I was better off keeping my mouth shut.

"You're worried about how people are going to look at you, but they'll look at you the same way you look at yourself. If you act like a whining little creep, everyone will think you're a whining little creep."

That sort of made sense and I nodded.

"Do you think it's easy for your Mom and Dad to be in the same place together?"

"No, they hate it," I said.

"They probably wish things were different, right?"

"For sure," I said. "Mom's always embarrassed."

"It's like she peed her pants in front of everyone, right?"

I started to laugh. Claire pulled me into a hug and I could smell strawberry ice cream on her breath.

"How'd you hit?" I asked.

"Three home runs," she said, "but my last time up, I struck out looking."

"You stink," I said.

She kissed me on the right cheek. I almost told her I loved her, but she already knew.

"Remember I told you to stand up for yourself?" she asked.

"Yeah, I guess I didn't do a very good job."

We started climbing down the tree. Claire jumped to the ground and looked back up at me.

"The best part of life is that you always get another chance," she said. "And always remember, when you fail, I'll be right by your side, making sure you get through it."

Chapter Four

- Clueless – May, 1988

"I was so naive as a kid I used to sneak behind the barn and do nothing." — Johnny Carson

When I was fifteen, Dad finally told me about the birds and the bees. I'm not sure how he figured it out, but he seemed to understand that Michael and I were more than a little curious about girls.

"Do either of you guys have a girl?" he asked.

I looked at Michael and up at Dad. I shook my father's question off.

"I'll tell you the secret," my father said.

He was acting as though he were the wisest man on the planet.

"Treat them with respect," he said.

I wanted to ask him if he thought cheating on Mom was respectful, but that was an old argument and we were all supposed to be over it.

"Worship their minds and bodies. Lay golden orchids at their feet. Cherish their spirit and appreciate that they're different. When other people are goading you into doing things that seem wrong, remember that women are people first, and objects of your desire second."

Thinking back on it, I'm not sure that my father actually said those words in that order. I'd like to think he appreciated Mom as a person, but I was probably terribly disillusioned. The problem was, I didn't have much time to think about it. I was about to embark on the first real sexual experience of my life.

◊ ◊ ◊

Dad's words of advise aside, I received a true education after meeting the new kid in town. Weird Henry Robinson moved into the trailer right next door to Steven. He instantly invaded our gang and I'll never forget the first conversation I ever had with him.

It was a painfully hot day at the end of June. Claire, Steven, Weird Henry and I were returning from a swimming hole in the back woods off Halley Road. Steven and Claire were laughing and flirting, as they always did. I was beyond worrying about it, but Weird Henry put a different spin on it as Claire and Steven ran ahead of us.

"They're doing it," Weird Henry said.

I had a vague idea of what he meant, but it wasn't true.

"Doing what?"

"*It*," he said. "Just look at them."

Claire was playfully slapping Steven's behind.

"They're friends," I said. I felt like I had swallowed my tongue.

"Get over it," Weird Henry said. "There's a lot of tail out there. Don't get caught up on one."

I hated the way he was referring to Claire. I also couldn't stand his cigarettes or his dirty clothes. He squinted at me as smoke billowed around his right eye.

"You want to get into her pants, don't you?"

I had never actually considered it. Claire was the love of my life. How could he make it sound so sleazy?

"No," I said. "God, she's my friend."

Claire and Steven were putting some distance between us. They were holding hands and swinging them wildly as they moved out of sight. Weird Henry was walking real slow, puffing on his disgusting cigarette. Having nowhere else to go, I walked by his side.

"You're kind of clueless, huh?" he said.

"No, of course not. What do you mean?" I asked.

Weird Henry was an odd-looking boy, but for one reason or another, I understood that he probably knew more about life than I did. I saw it as a learning experience, and I decided to play it cool.

"You know how old I was the first time I had sex?" Weird Henry asked.

"Can't say as I do," I said.

23

Weird Henry edged to the side of the road. He cleared away a couple of rocks and plopped down on the ground. Casually, I sat beside him. The sun was beating down hard, but I had a feeling that I was sweating for a very different reason.

"I was eleven," Weird Henry said. "My old man brought a stripper home, and when he was done with her, he paid for a session for me. He told me I needed to become a man."

"Get out," I said. "What kind of father would do that?"

"The kind that would shoot himself to death in our own house."

Weird Henry didn't look at me, and I couldn't be sure that he wasn't lying. I had so many questions. I wanted to know all about the stripper. I wanted to hear more about his father. Yet, Weird Henry didn't seem all that interested in talking about it.

"Do you even know what a woman looks like naked?" he asked.

I wanted to be a tough guy, but I didn't have much to say. I shrugged and looked down at my feet.

"I've seen women naked," I said.

Weird Henry picked a weed and started chewing on it. I peered down the road in search of Claire and Steven. How I wished they hadn't walked away.

"In the flesh?" Henry asked.

He spit the weed out and immediately lit another cigarette.

"In magazines," I said.

Michael had found one of Dad's magazines. We scanned it, but it was more upsetting than exciting.

"I know a girl who'll show you for real," Weird Henry said.

I turned away from him. This was getting strange, even for him.

"What do you say?" he asked.

Claire was completely out of sight, but I looked in her direction.

"You aren't going to get Claire," Weird Henry said. "I'll show you some-one closer to your league."

I wasn't sure what Weird Henry was trying to say, but there wasn't much I could do about any of it. I agreed to meet him at eight o'clock in front of his house.

◊ ◊ ◊

Weird Henry handed me a beer. I considered it for a moment and he jumped all over my hesitation.

"It's a twist-off," he said.

I hated the taste of beer, but what choice did I have? I turned the cap and it actually hurt my hand a little. Weird Henry eyed me suspiciously but he turned away after I gagged down a small swig.

"Where is she?" I asked.

"Patience, my man," Henry said.

We walked down the street and into the woods directly beyond the trailer lot. My stomach was a little queasy and I took another pull off the beer, hoping that would calm me down. I followed Weird Henry deep into the woods and he edged close to the creek and sat on a huge boulder. He pointed to a clearing directly across the stream.

"Grab another beer," he said, "Annette will be out in a minute. She agreed to meet us as long as we didn't get real close."

It didn't feel right. I shouldn't have been out there.

"She won't come out if you don't sit," Henry said.

Henry edged over on the rock and I reluctantly sat beside him.

"She's coming out naked?" I whispered.

"You don't have to whisper," Weird Henry said. "She's my girlfriend."

It still didn't add up.

"I told her you weren't sure what was going on and she agreed to model for me."

Weird Henry tapped me on the right shoulder. The sun was beginning to sink, but there was plenty of light. I was trying to figure out who Annette was when she stepped out of the clearing. She was wearing a string bikini and I had almost seen enough. Annette was a couple of years older than us. She smiled and waved.

"I'm doing her," Weird Henry said.

I couldn't imagine that he was treating her with much respect. She waved and then turned her back to us. Her right hand reached around to loosen the top strap. I tried to remain cool, but the anticipation was killing me. Weird Henry whistled crudely as she slipped her top off. I sipped the beer, not daring to move my eyes. Annette spun around and the sight of her breasts nearly knocked me over.

"Awesome, huh?" Weird Henry asked.

25

I was too tongue-tied to talk. Annette spun around and pulled her bottom down. I couldn't believe she was actually doing it. Weird Henry clapped wildly. I simply stared. Annette danced naked for us and although the show didn't last more than a few minutes, it caused a tremendous stir within my under-developed body.

I didn't sleep very much that night. Every time I closed my eyes, Annette was there, shaking her breasts in my face. What would make a girl do such a thing? I thought about the turmoil of my parents' divorce. I contemplated the feelings in my heart for Claire, but there wasn't anything that ever made me feel like Annette's naked body made me feel. I knew I would have to talk to someone, but whom? Michael wouldn't believe me; my mother would never let me out of the house again; it didn't seem right to talk to Claire; and my father would probably laugh. I drifted off to sleep with visions of nakedness running through my mind. Somehow, some way, I knew it was wrong.

The next morning, it was all out in the open. By the time Claire and Steven reached my house for our daily trek into the woods, word had spread like wild fire. Claire wasn't saying much, but Steven said that Weird Henry had been at his house with Annette and that they'd all had a good laugh over it.

"It's not true," I said lamely.

"Weird Henry said you were drooling all over yourself."

I tried to catch Claire's eye, but she looked away. When she lifted her head to meet my glance, I silently wished that I were blind. In her sparkling eyes, I saw the unmistakable look of disappointment.

The rest of my day was spent trying to control the damage. I stayed away from Michael and his probing questions. I dreaded the thought that Mom or Dad might find out and I locked myself in my room, vowing never to show my face in public again. Of course, in the middle of it all, Annette's naked body affected me as never before.

A few minutes before I collapsed under the weight of my shame, I heard a tapping on my window and a voice from outside. It was Claire in all her glory and she still wanted to talk to me!

Rather than risk being seen by a family member, I hoisted myself out the window. She eyed me rather sheepishly.

"Can we talk?" she asked.

I almost broke into tears. I was scared, ashamed and horrified.

"I'm sorry," I said.

"Let's walk and talk," she answered.

We walked deep into the woods. I can't explain it, but being alone with her was even more exciting than actually seeing Annette naked.

"I talked to Weird Henry," she said. "He admitted that he told you something about Steven and me that just isn't true."

I was a little confused. Why had she cornered Weird Henry? What made her responsible for me?

"Steven and I aren't doing it," she said. "I knew hearing something like that might upset you."

I dabbed at a tear.

"It still doesn't explain gawking at Annette," I said.

"Yeah, it kind of does," Claire said.

We stopped walking and she turned to face me. Our bodies were almost touching and our lips were inches apart. I tried to imagine what she looked like naked and something inside my head told me to stop it.

"There's a lot of stages in life," Claire said. "You shouldn't skip any."

She was talking in riddles and I always seemed to have trouble following her when she got deep on me.

"We're just kids. We shouldn't be doing adult things."

I kind of understood that, but she was teaching me a lesson and I needed to work harder to follow it.

"If life was perfect, we wouldn't be able to have children until we could raise them properly. We wouldn't ever know how to hate someone else. We'd be able to control our desires."

I didn't have a suitable response so I just stood there.

"You probably have a lot of weird thoughts in your head today."

I nodded and smiled.

"Don't ever let someone else cloud your vision of me," Claire said.

It looked as if she were about to cry, and for the first time, it occurred to me that she was disappointed in me as a friend. I had let her down by just accepting Weird Henry's proclamation as truth. I scanned the woods for a place to rest my eyes. I almost couldn't look at Claire for fear that I'd see that disappointment again.

"You're going to go through a lot in life," she said. "Your first kiss, or the excitement you feel when you hold a girl's hand for the first time. There's nothing like real love, but we're all just kids. It's not time for everything yet."

It didn't even feel like I was being lectured, but I was. I started to apologize again, but Claire pulled me close. Our lips met softly and her tongue slipped past my teeth. It was easily the most awesome feeling in the world. We held the kiss for what seemed like a hundred years.

When we broke our embrace, she smiled up at me.

"I figured it was time for that. I didn't want you doing it with just anyone."

Chapter Five

- The Ugliest Girl of All-Time – May, 1989

"My schoolmates would make love to anything that moved, but I never saw any reason to limit myself."
— *Emo Phillips*

Whoever coined the phrase "Sweet Sixteen" never saw me. I was tall and skinny with a face full of pimples. My classmates were all out having sex, or so they said, and I was struggling with the moral dilemma of having kissed my best friend's girl. I was still hopelessly in love with Claire and day after day, the world seemed gray. More than anything else, I was just plain listless. On a good day, I sat around watching television. On a bad day, I dreamed of finding someone who loved me for me. I couldn't catch a break.

Unfortunately, school dances and boy-girl socials are a way of life when you're sixteen years old. As the night of one such big dance approached, I searched for ways to avoid actually living.

"Are you washing your face regularly?" Mom asked as she set breakfast in front of me.

"Of course," I said.

She looked at Michael. "I don't know why he gets so many pimples." She was talking as if I weren't even in the room.

"He's a pizza face," Michael said. His skin was crystal clear and I hated him for it. Why had God signaled me out to carry this cross?

"Maybe you aren't rinsing the soap," she said. "Sometimes when you leave soap on your skin it becomes irritated."

"You can watch me wash," I said. "It's not a big deal."

I ran my hand over my left cheek. It *was* a big deal and I felt like crying.

"Maybe we'll get you some zit medicine," she said.

I had been through it all. I had soaked my face in enough cleansers to sink a ship. I had mud-caked my pores, heated my skin, and squeezed more pimples than I cared to count.

"Maybe if you cleared up his face, he could get a girl for the dance," Michael said.

"I don't want a stupid girl," I said. "Can we talk about something else?"

"Did you ask Claire about it?" Mom asked.

I put my fork down and glared at my mother. Why was she so comfortable humiliating me?

"Yeah, I asked her," I said, "but she said she loves me no matter what I look like."

I was trying to make a point, but it was lost on them.

"What the hell is she supposed to say?" Michael asked. "You're a hideous creature that stalks her. She's willing to say anything to keep you from jumping off a bridge."

My mother smiled. "I'll help you wash tonight."

◊ ◊ ◊

Brimming with confidence, I headed to school. My mother was going to stand beside me as I washed my freaking face! How could I even look at a girl with that sort of future hanging over my head?

The banner announcing the dance was strung along the school entrance. My hand instinctively went to my cheek. I would not be attending unless I was suddenly caught in a pimple medicine rainstorm.

"Hey, Leo," Weird Henry ambled towards me with a huge grin covering his perfectly opened pores. "Guess who got laid last night," he teased.

"Whatever," I said.

He followed my eyes to the banner.

"You going?" he asked.

"Doubt it," I said.

"I'll hook you up," he said.

"Don't worry about it."

30

I tried to twist by him and into the school.

"You have to go," he said. "Claire and Steven, me and Annette, your brother and Theresa. It'll be a blast."

"I don't have a date," I said. "Besides, I'm busy."

Weird Henry edged closer. He was blocking my path and to be honest, he was staring at me in a strange way.

"You know," he said, "I don't think you're rinsing the soap off your face right."

◊ ◊ ◊

That night, I lay in my bed daydreaming of how I could get Claire to love me. In the most pathetic of all fantasies, I dreamed that there was a huge fire in the cafeteria and that I carried student after student to safety. The firemen were screaming at me to stay back, but I returned to the fire once more to save Claire from sure death. As we collapsed on the front lawn of the school, with all the other students looking on, Claire wrapped her arms around me and pulled me close.

The knock on my door startled me back to reality and I sat up quickly as Mom entered carrying a bottle of zit medicine. Michael was right behind her.

"This stuff will clear you up," she said.

"He looks like the goalie for a dart team," Michael said.

Mom motioned Michael out the door. She sat on the edge of the bed and lightly spread the cream over the bumps and crevices on my skin. She brushed her lips lightly off the center of my forehead and tucked me into bed.

"In the morning everything will be fine," she whispered softly. "Any girl that doesn't want to go with you will be losing out."

I actually believed that I would wake up in the morning with perfectly clear skin. Of course, waking up pimple-free was as much of a dream as rescuing children from a burning school.

The next day, just after my first class, I ran into Claire in front of the library. The chances of running into her were good as I had memorized her class schedule, but I made it seem incidental.

"Leo, I've been looking for you all day," she said.

31

They were words that made my heart sing.

Claire grabbed my hand and pulled me to the wall. We watched the other kids pass and I imagined that we were boyfriend and girlfriend and everyone saw me with her.

"I have a date for you," Claire said.

I tried to fake a smile. Her eyes danced across my blemished face.

"You like Stephanie, right?"

Stephanie was Claire's biggest, fattest friend. I actually couldn't stand the girl, but I pretended, for Claire's sake.

"Oh yeah," I said. "She doesn't have a date?"

"No, and she asked me to see if you'd go with her."

I had hit rock bottom. Not only was everyone trying to get me a date but now the quality of girl had reached an all-time low.

"I don't think so," I said.

Claire didn't bother to hide her disappointment.

"After all the favors I've done for you," she said. She turned away, and I know, deep in her heart, she understood that I would never let her walk away.

"All right," I said.

◊ ◊ ◊

The teasing was almost unbearable. Michael showed Stephanie's picture to Mom and Dad, and as we prepared for the dance, everyone had a great laugh at my expense. It was especially distressing when I reached into the side pocket of my suit coat and pulled out a handful of dog biscuits.

"I thought you might need those," Michael said. "In case you want her to do some tricks or something."

"We're going as friends," I said, but that still didn't take the sting away.

Stephanie was every bit of a hundred-sixty pounds. She wore thick, coke bottle glasses, and her zits made my zits look like baby pimples.

"I'm sure she's a nice girl," Mom said.

We met in our front yard. Claire and Steven looked like a million bucks. Michael and Theresa were dashing and charming. Even Weird Henry and Annette appeared to have a small degree of dignity. It was Stephanie and poor Leo who looked the most pitiful.

"You look nice," Stephanie said.

The zit in the center of her forehead looked like a third eye.

"So do you," I said.

She pinned a flower on my lapel and I returned the favor.

"Thank you for asking me," she said. "I know that wasn't easy to do."

And so started the biggest pity party of all-time.

We danced a couple of times, but mostly we tried to hang around with the couples that truly belonged there. I pretended that I was Claire's date and Stephanie pretended that she wasn't hurt by my inattention.

However, the end of the night found us alone. We sat on the front steps of the school. The other couples were making out or worse. We just had words to soothe us.

"You know what really bothers me?" Stephanie asked.

"What's that?" I asked.

"It's not that I don't fit in. I couldn't care less what other people think of me."

The night was deathly quiet and I wished I were anywhere else in the world.

"But I'm not stupid. I get perfect grades, you know," she said.

I hadn't known that, but I don't know why that mattered anyway.

"I know I'm fat and painfully ugly."

She said it without a trace of regret. In fact, I almost laughed at her brutal honesty.

"Don't tell me I'm not, either," she said. "People always do that. My parents always tell me how beautiful I am, but I have a fucking mirror. I know."

Suddenly, it wasn't all about me anymore.

"I just wonder why we're born the way we are. I'm fat, you got pimples and Steven and Claire are visually perfect."

I shrugged, but I couldn't come up with anything.

"I have a confession," she said. She placed a beefy hand on my right leg. "I'm as much in love with Steven as you are with Claire. Yet, what does that get us?"

"Nothing," I said.

Stephanie laughed boisterously.

"Claire said Michael filled your coat pockets with dog biscuits."

33

I took out a couple of biscuits and offered her one. She took it without hesitation.

"The thing is, some day those looks will go away," she said.

She twirled the biscuit around in her hand. She didn't seem able to look me in the eye. "Or maybe, your skin will clear up and I'll lose weight and get rid of these freaking glasses."

"Maybe the sky will fall too," I said.

We both laughed. Stephanie held the biscuit to her nose.

"Some day we'll all be even. Maybe I'll even be happier than Claire. Who knows?"

She licked the biscuit and then smiled at me as she took a bite.

"Why do dogs love these fucking things so much?" she asked.

Stephanie was the second girl that I ever kissed.

Chapter Six

– Easy – April, 1991

"A relationship is what happens between two people who are
waiting for something better to come along." — Unknown

If you haven't experienced a Buffalo winter, you haven't actually lived.
From the middle of December on through to early March, the snow flies,
the days are short and dark, and its almost unfathomable to understand
that summer is coming. As a rite of spring, high school seniors dream of
taking a break in a warm climate. At eighteen years old, I was just sort of
drifting through life. Every time that a discussion about the future came
up, I wanted to run and hide. I hadn't yet done anything in life, but I sure
needed a vacation.

I grabbed my lunch tray and muddled through the food line. Steven
was in front of me, and Weird Henry was close behind. As we shared lunch
each and every day, I was certain that Claire was already waiting for us at
the usual table.

"Are you doing anything for spring break?" Steven asked.

I shrugged. I grabbed a small container of chocolate milk and moved
forward.

"I'm getting sick of the weather," Steven said. "The sun hasn't been
around for months. Now we have two nice days in a row, and it'll probably
rain for another week. Let's get out of here."

Just as he did each and every day, Weird Henry ordered a peanut but-
ter and jelly sandwich.

"We should go to Florida for spring break," Weird Henry said. "We get like a week off for Easter and that's when the shit is really happening down there."

"I'd love to go," I said.

Steven was at the register. He turned to face me and I could see the wheels spinning in his mind. He was our leader, and if there were a chance to pull this off, he'd be the one to make it work.

"Let's do it," he said.

"Yeah, maybe we can get Leo laid," Weird Henry said.

My inability to make it with a member of the opposite sex was something that everyone, with the possible exception of Claire, found amusing.

By the time I set my tray on the lunch table, Steven had straightened it all out.

"I'll call a travel agent and get the hotel room, and we can drive my car. We'll lie on the beach, have a few drinks and let off a little steam before we head off into real life. We deserve this."

Steven explained the plan in full detail. Although it began as a trip that Michael, Claire and Weird Henry would be making, life slowly interfered.

"It's a great idea," Claire said, "but I'm taking college classes at Buffalo State. I can't go."

"Michael can't get a break either," I said. "He just started his job."

All eyes turned to Weird Henry. He was already shaking us off.

"I don't have any bread," he said.

I took a bite of the cardboard-like pizza.

"Ah, well, it *was* a good idea," I said.

We were silent for quite awhile. Finally, Claire said what I was thinking.

"Why can't you and Steven go?"

I looked at him hopefully. I wasn't quite sure that he'd want to be stuck with me for a week in Florida.

"Can you get money?" Steven asked.

"I can try," I said.

Although the trip would have been complete had Claire been able to come along, I was still thrilled to be entertaining the idea.

"Yeah, maybe you can get a little," Weird Henry said.

Claire shot him a dirty look and I smiled at her, realizing that she always watched my back.

"It's a twenty-two hour trip," Steven said, "and if we split the drive, we can go straight through."

As an adult, you'd never consider such lunacy, but it was the perfect trip for a couple of eighteen-year olds.

Looking for permission, I decided to attack my father's sensibilities first. Earlier in the year, Dad had married Margaret. While it was a choice that meant very little to me, he was extremely worried about my feelings.

The ironic part of it all was that the next day was an unusually warm one. I took advantage of the three days without rain by cutting the massive lawn behind Dad and Margaret's new, little home. Margaret was home alone when I got there, and I realized that I would have to pretend to like her. I wasn't big on cutting lawn, but, hey, kissing ass is kissing ass.

When I was finished, Margaret appeared with a pitcher of lemonade. I had mowed the lawn with my shirt off, in hopes of getting a tan, but I pulled the shirt on before ambling up to her. I didn't want her judging my scrawny chest.

"Your father's going to be thrilled," Margaret said. She poured a glass of lemonade and pushed it towards me. I sat across from her at the picnic table.

"That's the first time the lawn has been mowed here. Every time he thought about cutting it, it rained. It looks good."

I had precious little to say to her, but I did my best.

"It's a great house; you guys must be proud," I said.

Margaret smiled and I looked directly into her brown eyes, wondering why my father would leave a perfectly good woman for her.

"It feels like home," Margaret said. "When we first got together, there was something missing. Now, it feels like he's all mine."

It took a lot for me to ignore the statement, but I did. I had Florida to consider and I wasn't about to blow it by pissing off Margaret. Thankfully, Dad came around the back corner of the house and sat beside her. He leaned in and kissed her and she groaned as though his kiss was a medicine.

"I see you mowed the lawn," Dad said. "Does this have anything to do with wanting to go to Florida?"

37

Clifford Fazzolari

I couldn't figure out how he had discovered my intentions, but he cleared it up for me.

"Your mother called to mention that you were thinking about it. Has she said yes?"

"Not yet," I answered. I sipped the lemonade, which was way too sweet.

"So, what do you want from me?" Dad asked.

I figured I'd get right to the point. Dad always seemed ready to compensate us for leaving, and coming right at him usually worked best.

"Your permission and two hundred bucks," I said.

Both Dad and Margaret laughed.

"Tell me what your plan is," he said.

Dad draped his arm around Margaret's shoulder and she began caressing his biceps. It was almost enough to make me vomit.

"We're taking Steven's car. It's real dependable and we already got maps and everything. The travel agent booked a hotel for us, and we even got a meal plan, if we want it."

"And you're going to drink heavily, right?" Dad asked.

"No, we're going to meet people. You know, hang out."

There was a sparkle in my father's eyes and I recognized it as a start of one of his yarns from days gone by.

"Your mother and I went to Florida when we were eighteen," he said.

I was sure Margaret didn't want to hear the story, but she hung right in there, the nosy bitch.

"We had a great time."

Margaret giggled and playfully tugged at my father's shirtsleeve. "I bet you got laid, didn't you?"

Now, I could put up with a lot of nonsense, but Margaret joking about my mother was over the line. I pushed the glass to the center of the table and jumped from my chair.

"Oh, I was only kidding," Margaret said.

"I've got to go," I said.

It was the perfect hook and Dad swallowed it. He extracted his wallet and laid ten twenty-dollar bills on the table.

"You have my permission and my money, but if your mother doesn't agree, I'm pulling my permission back. You can keep the money. Remem-

38

ber, Mom's a lonely woman, and with Michael away at school, you're all she has left."

The entire thing gnawed at me, but I pocketed the money. Since the divorce, there were times when I couldn't stand what my father represented, but he was always capable of a new low. I wanted to tell him that he was the reason Mom was lonely. She had sacrificed everything for us while he played house with the lovely Margaret. But, why blow a good thing? I thanked him for the money. He made a lame joke about how expensive it was to get his grass cut, and I feigned laughter. Fuck him.

◊ ◊ ◊

A couple of hours later, I met Steven at his house to go over the particulars. We had nearly eight hundred dollars, a map detailing the trip, and a cooler filled with soda and sandwiches. We were going to golf, swim, look at girls, eat great food, and yes, drink a few beers.

"All we have to do now is get your mother to agree," Steven said.

"Let's head over there," I said. "If she goes for it, we can leave early tomorrow."

We were so confident that Mom would agree that we packed Steven's car before heading over. I wish it would've taken us a little longer.

There was a strange car in the driveway, but I didn't give it a second glance.

"Maybe she's got company," Steven said.

I waved him off and used my key to open the front door. At that instant, my world stopped spinning. My mother was lying on the couch, naked, with a strange man, also naked, on top of her. I dropped the keys and felt Steven's push out the front door. I sat on the stoop in a state of complete shock. Steven was trying to comfort me, but what could he say?

After about twenty minutes, they emerged from the house. They acted as though everything was just perfect, but when Mom introduced me to Keith, her eyes were nowhere to be found. Keith backed down the driveway. I hoped that he'd be involved in a head-on collision on his way to wherever the hell he was going.

"So, what's up?" Mom asked as though we'd walked in while she was finishing up the laundry.

39

"Florida," Steven said. "We're all set to go. We just need your blessing."

Mom eyed us suspiciously but I still couldn't look her in the face.

"You're still my baby boy," she said.

Steven smiled, and I thought that I might die of embarrassment.

"Will you call every night?" she asked.

"Absolutely," Steven said.

She opened her arms for me. I realized that I wasn't going to get away without hugging her, but the thought of her with Keith nearly stopped me.

"You grew up too fast," she said. She hugged me tightly, and I nearly cried in her arms.

Although she could ill-afford it, she took twenty bucks out of her purse and handed it to me. I kissed her on the cheek.

"Just take care of yourself," she said.

I barely heard her. Deep down, I understood that catching her making love was more than I could handle.

"We're going to Florida!" Steven said.

We slapped hands and headed for the car.

◊ ◊ ◊

We jumped on I-90 and traveled through Erie, Pennsylvania towards I-79. Steven took the first turn at driving, and true to the nature of our friendship, he immediately brought up my mother.

"She's been alone a long time," he said. "She's a nice-looking woman. You know, those things are bound to happen."

But I didn't know. It was my mother, for God's sake.

"I'm so confused I don't know anything," I said. "It's three months before graduation, and I don't know what the hell I'm going to do with my life."

Steven alternated looks between the road and me. He took a healthy chug of soda. He was a great guy whose future was all mapped out. He had an athletic scholarship to Canisius, the best girl in the world, and more than his share of good looks.

"You'll be all right," he said. "You just have to remember that life does-n't always come to you. Sometimes you have to go out and get it."

"I don't know," I said. "Maybe it was the divorce, but for some reason, I feel like I'm always on my heels. It's like I'm waiting for bad things to happen."

Steven considered it for a moment. A smile creased his lips.

"I have Claire to keep me straight," he said. "She's always telling me that bad things can happen, but that you have to meet them head-on."

I slumped down in the seat. The sun was playing havoc with my ability to look straight ahead. I closed my eyes and quickly drifted towards sleep. I wasn't sure that I wanted to think about it all that much.

When I awoke, Steven was softly singing along with the radio.

"How was your nap?" he asked.

I stretched out.

"Where are we?" I asked.

"Almost to West Virginia," he said.

He was smiling again, and it struck me that I didn't know a happier person. Yet, why wouldn't he be happy? Claire was in love with him.

"I have an uncle who always tells us the same joke about visiting West Virginia," Steven said. He giggled again.

"What's that?" I asked. I reached into the cooler and fished out another soda.

"He says that one time he was in West Virginia and this guy came up to him and said, 'I'd like you to meet my wife and my sister.'"

"Yeah," I said.

"My uncle says that there was only one girl standing there."

It took me a minute, but I joined him in laughter.

"I have to tell you something," he said.

His smile dimmed, and I realized that what he was about to say was going to be real painful.

"What's wrong?" I asked.

"Nothing. It's just that Claire and me, uh, decided to get married."

I'm not sure what I was trying to accomplish, but I pretended I didn't hear him.

"What's that?" I asked.

"We're getting married," he said.

41

I rubbed my face with my right hand. The radio was playing an old Springsteen song, and I concentrated on the lyrics, pretending that if I made him say it three times, it wouldn't be true.

"We both have athletic scholarships and jobs that'll pay us enough money to get by until school's over," Steven said.

He glanced at me, but I looked away. I opened the window and breathed deep, actually feeling the air fill my lungs. I was sure that even a gun to my head wouldn't bring about the ability to speak.

"We've always loved each other," Steven said.

I gulped at the air once more.

"We don't want to be with anyone else and there's no reason to wait," he said.

It was my worst nightmare coming true. I took a swig of soda, but I coughed it up, all over the dashboard. I started wiping at the mess, but Steven gripped my hand. He was looking at the road, but his grasp on my wrist was almost painful.

"I need you to react," he whispered.

"I'm reacting," I said. "I'm choking to death."

We traveled in silence for a few minutes. I knew that I was being self-ish, but so were they. What was going to happen to me? The Springsteen song gave way to a Rolling Stones ballad, and I felt like crying my eyes out.

"I've always loved her, too," I said.

Steven still hadn't let go of my wrist. He gripped it a little more tenderly.

"I know," he said.

"I always thought she'd be my wife."

Steven shook his head in pity. It was the first time that I actually disliked him for anything.

"It'll happen for you, someday," he said.

But he couldn't understand that I didn't want it to happen with anyone else. Claire was always right there for me. She loved me when no one else did, and now, she'd be gone forever.

"Couldn't we all get married?" I asked.

Steven playfully punched me in the left arm. He had no idea how much it really hurt.

◊ ◊ ◊

We slept for a while at rest stops in North Carolina and Georgia. My mind was a whirlwind of thought. First, I concentrated on my mother in the missionary position with some disgusting man, and then, I thought of Claire and Steven making love on a blanket beneath the stars. I actually thought of getting out of the back seat and walking off into the woods, never to be heard from again.

Yet I couldn't do it. Who was I to say that my mother couldn't be happy? Or Claire and Steven, for that matter? What right did I have being a baby just because I was pathetic?

When we crossed the border into Florida, we clapped hands as though we'd landed on the moon. Steven wasn't a bad guy just because he loved my woman.

"I want you to know that we'll always be best buddies," he said. "No matter what happens, we'll be side-by-side forever."

Again, I wanted to cry. It wasn't that what he said touched me so deeply; it was because I knew it wouldn't go down that way. He'd marry Claire, they'd have a couple of kids, and they'd say, "I wonder what happened to that poor bastard, Leo."

"There's no doubt about it," I said, "best friends forever."

◊ ◊ ◊

We settled into our room at a little after three in the afternoon. The weather was cooperating nicely, as it was eighty-four and sunny. The beach was just a short walk out our back door, and the first beer tasted great. The problem was that we didn't have a clue as to where we should go.

Steven lay back on the bed, kicking his shoes to the floor. He clicked on the television set and cranked up MTV.

I started laughing. "Please don't tell me we drove thirteen hundred miles to watch television," I said.

He tossed a pillow at me. I sat on the edge of the bed and peeled the label off my beer bottle. The shock of the impending wedding was starting to wear off, but the pain in my heart wouldn't go away.

43

"Do you really believe in marriage?" I asked.

Steven turned the volume down.

"It is sort of scary, isn't it?" he asked. "I mean there are millions of girls out there."

"Yeah, why would you want just one?" I asked.

"But Claire is my girl," he said.

"That's a good point," I said.

I sipped the beer, and nearly commented about how good it was.

"My Mom and Dad can barely look at each other anymore," I said.

"They're better off than Weird Henry's old man," Steven said.

"I know, he told me about that," I said.

Steven raised his beer high. He offered a salute to Weird Henry.

"You really have to be up against it to kill yourself. Weird Henry always says that his old lady nagged the poor guy to death."

I drained the beer and reached for another.

"Man, when he told me, I thought he was joking," I said.

"Who'd joke about something like that?" Steven asked. "Life can get ugly. Hey, toss me another beer."

I threw him the beer and he caught it without even looking in my direction. I'd have given my left arm to be as cool as Steven.

"I'm still a virgin," I said.

I wanted him to say that he was, too.

He closed his eyes.

"I want to get laid tonight," I said.

Steven clicked MTV into oblivion.

"Let's go then," he said.

◊ ◊ ◊

Four hours later, we were seated at the counter of a place called the *Captain's Cove*. There were fishnets hanging from the walls, the draft beer was seventy cents a glass, and the place was wall-to-wall with women in bikinis. I thought I was going to sprain my neck looking around the place, and Steven laughed every time that I proclaimed my love for a wandering lovely.

"You feel like going somewhere to eat?" Steven asked.

I was just starting another glass of beer and a redhead with the biggest breasts I'd ever seen was standing in my line of vision.

"I'm not going anywhere," I said.

The bartender wiped the area in front of us and grinned at me.

"It's a great place to work," he said.

I imagined myself working in such a place, and I figured that sooner or later, I'd find something to whine about.

"We have live lobsters in the tank," the bartender said. "Pick one out and we'll cook it up for you."

We moved to the tank with our beer in hand. Steven told the guy that any one would be fine, but I carefully considered my choices, changing my mind seven times. I was concentrating so hard that I never even noticed the girl standing to my immediate right. She peered into the tank. Every once in awhile, she looked at me.

"We'll take that one, and the one right next to it," she said.

I snapped my head around and immediately took stock in what she had under her string bikini. She was a brunette, about five-four, and a hundred pounds. The sun had turned her skin dark brown, but her eyes were even darker. My first thought was that she'd do nicely for what I had in mind, and my second thought was, why the hell is she talking to me?

"My name's Lane," she said.

"Like lover's lane?" I asked.

She tossed her head back and offered a truly terrific laugh that made my stomach queasy.

"Exactly," she said.

She was drinking something with an umbrella in it and I offered to buy her one.

"That'd be great," she said, "but I have to use the ladies room first."

I pointed to our seats at the bar and she shook and shimmied her way to the bathroom. Steven patted me on the back and laughed. We were in full glee when the bartender joined us.

"You met Lane, huh?" he asked.

Here it comes, I thought. Lane was really a man, or, she was recently paroled from jail after robbing a series of banks and killing the tellers.

"Yeah, she seems nice," I said.

"She is nice," the bartender said. "A little too nice. We call her *Easy*. I've been working here six months and she's probably slept with thirty men."

I took that bit of news with a glint of enthusiasm. What did I care?

"Oh," Steven said.

"She's a stripper at *Solid Gold*. It's right down the street. Her real name is Erin."

The bartender set Lane or Erin or *Easy* up with a drink, and I battled myself for a strategy. I had less than a minute to decide. When we spotted her coming from the rest room, Steven whispered softly in my ear.

"She's going to be trouble," he said.

Yet, what was I supposed to do? Steven had Claire. Michael had Theresa. Weird Henry had Annette. My father had Margaret. My mother had Keith. I wanted someone. What could possibly go wrong?

I battled that lobster for all that I was worth, and it would have been a losing battle had Lane not been there. She showed me how to pluck the meat out, and she did it with the most amazing smile. The scent of her perfume was driving me crazy, and every time our hands touched, that unbelievable wave of desire swept through my body. Steven was a spectator to all of it, but he kept the drinks coming, and allowed me to make my own mistakes.

"So, do you have a girlfriend?" Lane asked.

"Not really," I said.

I didn't want to tell her that I hadn't had so much as a date in the past six months. In any regard, she laughed.

"What do you mean, not really? Either you do or you don't, right?"

I tried to appear casual as I fought for a piece of meat buried underneath the shell.

"Well, there's someone that I'm interested in, but she's marrying him."

Steven had his back to us, and Lane's eyes traveled up and down his body.

"Some guys have all the luck," she said.

The desire sweeping through my body was almost too much for me to handle. I took a swig of beer and smiled at Lane as though she were a present under the tree on Christmas morning.

"You're a small town boy, aren't you?" Lane asked.

"No, I'm from Buffalo," I said.

She laughed, but I wasn't sure why it was funny.

"You have a real innocence," she said.

The bartender cleared our plates. I brushed the remnants of the lobster from my lap.

"I'm sick of being innocent," I said.

She smiled again, and pulled on her drink through a straw. Her eyes never left my face and her right hand found my bare thigh.

"I wish I didn't have to work tonight," she said.

She had no idea that I knew where she worked.

"What time are you done?" I asked.

"It'll be late," she said.

I swallowed hard. This was the important part. Somehow, I had to get her to meet me.

"I'm on vacation," I said. "There's no such thing as time."

She actually turned in her chair so she wouldn't have to look at me.

"You're too nice of a guy," she said.

I didn't want to be nice. Why couldn't anyone see that?

"I'm here for a week," I said. "I want to see you again."

When she turned to face me, there were tears in her eyes.

"It's probably not a good idea," she said. "We're from different worlds. I don't want to bring you down."

She leaned in, kissed me on the forehead, grabbed the check for our dinners, and left me sitting there with my mouth wide open.

◊ ◊ ◊

We had a couple more beers, but my heart wasn't in it. Steven tried to take my mind off of it by beating the hell out of me in darts and pool. In the grand scheme of things, I just didn't measure up in anything.

At a little after midnight, we left *Captain's Cove* and headed back towards the hotel. The stars were burning brightly in the black of a perfectly clear night. The sand beneath our feet was difficult to walk in and I was doing more sliding than walking. I didn't want to be in Florida with Steven by my side. I wanted to be holding someone's hand, whether it be Lane's, or Claire's, or even my Mom's. It was an important night, and I knew it. There's was no getting around the fact that I was pretty much on my own, and I needed to find my way.

"Tomorrow we'll head down to the beach and catch some sun," Steven said. "I'll look through some of the brochures at the front desk to find us a decent golf course."

"Man, I've just about had it," I said. "I'm just sitting here waiting for my life to begin. I'm sick of waiting for the train to come around the bend."

Steven draped an arm around my shoulder.

"You're a good guy," he said. "Good things will happen for you."

"She liked me," I said.

I stopped walking just a few hundred feet from the hotel.

"I'm going to *Solid Gold*," I said.

"I don't think you want to see that," Steven said.

"I *have* to," I said.

I started to back-pedal away.

"All right, hang on, I'll go with you," he said.

◊ ◊ ◊

When we walked in, Lane was on stage. She was completely naked, and poised over the top of a fat businessman, who held a dollar in his mouth. I turned away and Steven ushered me to the bar.

We ordered two beers and a drink with an umbrella in it. I sat, with my back to the stage, unable to look at Lane's naked gyrations. I thought of watching Annette with Weird Henry, and I wondered about how it all seemed so complicated now. I know that Steven was really battling his own sensibilities, but he wouldn't look at Lane either. Thankfully, two songs later, it was over. A new dancer was introduced and Lane skipped off the stage to thunderous applause.

Five minutes later, she was seated beside me.

◊ ◊ ◊

We walked the same section of beach that Steven and I had walked. Her left hand was coupled with my right, and it felt better than I had dreamed.

"You know what I love more than anything?" she asked.

48

"Lobster?" I said.

She laughed again, and playfully swung our coupled hands in front of us.

"I love sunsets, but most of all, I love to watch the stars come out. When I was a little girl, I used to sneak out of the house and watch the sky fill up with stars."

She was looking skyward as though her entire existence depended upon it.

"So, what's your story?" I asked.

"What do you mean?"

"I don't know. You saw my innocence. I'm just guessing that there's something going on with you."

She led me down the beach to the water's edge. The waves were moving slowly to the shore. Lane slipped off her shoes and buried her toes in the wet sand.

"My father beat me," she said.

"What's that?" I asked.

"I was about ten when it started," she said. "He liked whiskey better than me."

I felt the sand and water between my toes. Perhaps she had been right. This was way out of my realm of understanding.

"He was always slapping or punching me. My mother ran out on him and I hated her for leaving me there, but she was scared to death, too."

She started to cry, and I pulled her to my chest.

"I ran away two years ago. I was only sixteen, but all my dreams were gone."

She wiped at her pretty eyes, and tried to smile through the tears.

"I couldn't live like that anymore," she said.

We sat on the water's edge. I hated her father and all the men like him.

"I knew I'd be able to dance for a living, but my chances for a normal life were shot."

We kissed softly and slowly at first, and hungrily and desperately soon after.

"All of the bruises are inside now," she said.

We parted company a little after seven in the morning. Eventually, we had made love. My life would never be the same. But I doubt if the experience changed things for her.

When I returned to Buffalo, I wrote her a letter every day for a week. I never heard from *Easy* again.

Chapter Seven

– What are you going to do with your life?
– June, 1991

"Your chances of getting hit by lightning go up if you stand under a tree, shake your fist at the sky, and say 'Storms Suck!'"
— *Johnny Carson*

It was less than a month to the day of my high school graduation and I still didn't have a clue as to what I'd be doing come September. In the cruelest of all twists, I would not be returning to my high school for another year of chasing Claire. In those days, I was spending less and less time being influenced by my parents, but I was slightly remiss in thinking that they didn't have anything to say about the course of my life. It all started with a phone call.

"Hey," Dad said. "What're you doing tonight?"

Of course, I didn't have any plans, but I couldn't let him know that.

"I'm going out with some friends," I said.

"Why don't you swing by here," Dad said. "We'll have a couple of beers. You've got time for your old man, don't you?"

The idea of hanging out with my father didn't thrill me, but it was either he or Weird Henry, and at least Dad would pay for the beer.

"Yeah, I'll stop by," I said.

He was waiting for me in the back yard. There was a twelve-pack of Budweiser in the center of the picnic table. Dad opened one and slid it across to me. It didn't take him long to get to his point.

"What colleges have you looked at?" he asked.

"I got accepted to a couple," I said.

He raised his bottle to mine and the glass clanged as we saluted my good fortune.

"I know you like sports," he said. "You've always been interested in that."

I took a healthy swig of beer. Something about drinking with my father made me feel more like a man.

"Problem is, there's not much call for a slow-footed, weak-hitting second baseman in the professional ranks," I said.

He laughed and raised his bottle yet again. For the second time, we touched our beers together.

"No, I was thinking about something behind the scenes," he said. "Like a statistician or a writer or something."

Whether he knew it or not, he was dead on the money. My dream job would be to cover a professional sports team on a daily basis.

"I don't know," I said. "In case you haven't noticed, I've been a little confused about what direction to take."

I sipped the beer again. It was going down easy, but I didn't want to chug it as though I were drinking beside Weird Henry.

"I've noticed," he said.

Now, as way of clarification, my relationship with my father had never been truly healthy. I was well aware of the fact that he was prying into my life where before he had never taken much of an interest.

"How about girls?" he asked. "Michael's got a nice one. Theresa's a real fine lady."

He paused as though he were considering their future together.

"She kind of reminds me of your Mom at that age," he said.

I drained the beer from the bottle. Suddenly, I didn't really give a shit about how quickly I was drinking. I immediately reached for another.

"Michael is doing an excellent job in school, too. Do you know how much money an architect makes in a year?" Dad asked.

I struggled with the cap, and Dad took the bottle from me and twisted it open.

"You need a trade of some sort," he said, "or this world will eat you up."

Suddenly, I wished I were anywhere else but sitting across from him. I decided to throw a little bit back in his direction.

"One thing I don't want to do is pick the wrong girl," I said. "I'd hate to start a family and then have to leave it."

The color drained from his face. He held the bottle to his lips, but shook his head before taking a sip.

"That's what I'm getting at," he said. "You don't know jack-shit about anything."

"I'm just talking," I said.

He shook his head again as though I were the dumbest man on the face of the planet.

"Some day you'll know what it's like to have a relationship," he said. "At least I hope you will."

I shrugged and slammed down half my second beer in one large gulp.

"I'd rather *not* have one than screw one up," I said.

He slammed his fist on the table. The twelve-pack actually bounced in place.

"I hope you become a man someday," he said.

He was in a full-fledged rage, and I honestly couldn't blame him.

"Don't worry about it. I'll become a man," I said.

"Yeah, maybe," he said, "but I'll probably be dead before that happens."

He stormed off towards the house and I grabbed the remaining nine beers. All in all, it hadn't worked out too badly. I was still going to get to drink with Weird Henry, and my father paid for the beer.

◊ ◊ ◊

I walked through the woods to Weird Henry's house. Normally, he wasn't real thrilled about letting me into his home, but I didn't have much of a choice. I needed a drinking partner. It was easy to see that Weird Henry's family was well below the poverty level. Weird Henry lived with his mother in a trailer home, and the reason he didn't want me in the house was because of their meager surroundings.

Weird Henry answered the door just before my third knock. The cigarette dangled out of his mouth as he told me to come in.

"What's up?" I asked.

He noticed the beer in my hand.

"Nice," he said. "Give me one of those fuckers."

I tossed him a beer and took a quick look around. There was a beat-up old couch in one corner and a small television set with wire ears for an antenna.

"I fell asleep after dinner," Weird Henry said. "I wondered what you were doing."

He opened the beer and guzzled half of it.

"I was with my father," I said. "It sucked."

Weird Henry flopped on the couch. The ash fell from his cigarette onto the carpet and he rubbed it in with his foot.

"See that chair over there?" he asked.

There was an old beat-up recliner in one corner of the room. It was an odd piece of furniture because if you sat in it, you were at a bad angle to see the television. It was draped with an old, stained bed sheet.

"What about it?" I asked.

"That's where my old man shot himself," he said.

I looked at the chair and back at Henry, but he didn't seem at all phased by his proclamation.

"I found him when I came home from school one day."

"Jesus, that's awful," I said.

Weird Henry was on his feet heading towards his cigarettes and the beer.

"That's life," he said. "My old man was too good for this world. Fuck it. I don't want to talk about it."

But, I wanted to hear all about it. I needed him to describe it to me.

"When did it happen?" I asked.

"Just after we moved here," he said. "We told everyone it was a heart attack. He put the gun in his mouth and pulled the trigger. It really wasn't a big deal."

I was looking at the chair as though it would come to life and bite me.

"We don't sit in it anymore," he said. "It's kind of like Archie Bunker's chair in the Smithsonian."

Weird Henry laughed, and I wasn't exactly sure what was funny.

"Thing is, the old man lost faith in the world. When I think about it, he wasn't really gutless as my mother says. He had the guts to get out of a bad spot."

"I'm not sure that's a way out," I said.

"That's because you still have the faith," he said.

He took a passing glance at the chair, grabbed the rest of the beer, and headed for the door. We took our normal path back through the woods and along the railroad tracks that lead into town if you cared to travel that far.

"What do you see yourself doing in ten years?" Weird Henry asked.

The sun was making its descent and I dared to look right into it. My vision was starting to blur, but I could not be deterred. I opened another beer and skipped a rock into the woods.

"That's a great question," I said.

"Let me guess for you," Weird Henry said.

I took a healthy swig of the beer. It was a game I wasn't sure that I wanted to play, but what the hell else was there to do?

"You'll be stuck in a nowhere job, with two kids and a wife," he said.

I laughed at his vision of me.

"How the hell will I get a wife?" I asked.

"She'll be bone ugly," Weird Henry said. "You'll have knocked her up in the back seat of some car, and you'll marry her to shut her up."

"Wonderful," I said.

"Seriously," he said. "You're too nice of a guy to just walk away from a broad in need."

The discussion was going nowhere. Yet, as if probing a sore in my mouth with my tongue, I kept it going.

"What kind of job will I have?" I asked.

"Menial," he said. "You'll be too wimpy to take advantage of any opportunities, and too scared to take any chances."

Not exactly a ringing endorsement, but what did Weird Henry know?

"What about you?" I asked.

"Oh, I'll be dead," he said.

It was a horrendous thought, but there wasn't anything in his voice that told me he believed otherwise.

"I'm thinking a car accident," he said. "I'll be alone and drunk, and I'll tip the car over on my way to a better place."

I finished the rest of my beer and peeled the label away.

"That's horrible," I said. "How can you even talk like that?"

Weird Henry took a drag on his cigarette.

"I'm not sure," he said. "But if you spend your time worrying about what's going to happen to you in ten years, you'll never live your life the right way. What if I plan everything out and then I croak? What's the sense of worrying about it?"

That sort of made sense, but in a strange way, I knew that Weird Henry was way off the mark.

"The problem with death," I said, "is you don't know what happens."

"That's true," he said. "But, the problem with life is that you do."

We walked and talked for a while, and then I headed back to the house. I needed to have some kind of future. As we parted company for the night, Weird Henry called out to me.

"Keep the faith. Be a college boy. You'll be fine."

I could only pray he was right.

◊ ◊ ◊

My mother, bless her heart, saved money for my education. In fact, she filled out a number of applications and three weeks before graduation, she broke the news to me.

"Next Saturday we'll visit schools. You'll decide from there what you're going to do."

So, there it was. My mother made my decisions for me. I didn't have a reasonable argument, so I just nodded. The night before we were to visit Gannon University in Erie, Pennsylvania and the State University of New York at Fredonia, I lay in bed wishing there was a way I could shape a life worth living. I couldn't get the thought of Weird Henry's father out of my mind. The argument with Dad also kept resonating in my brain.

Of course, Claire answered the call by tossing a couple of stones off my bedroom window. I climbed out the window and met her on the front lawn.

"Hey, you," she said.

She gave me a hug and a quick kiss on the cheek. I got a whiff of her perfume and it made my heart jump.

"I was walking back from Steven's," she said. "I decided to pay you a visit."

"Just in the nick of time, like always," I said.

We walked a little ways and sat on the lawn across from my house.

"What's up?" she said.

She patted my knee as if I were a child. She smiled that gorgeous smile and edged closer. The night was obviously dark, but it was as if I were seeing her in brilliant sunshine.

"I'm worried about visiting colleges tomorrow," I said.

"It's a piece of cake," Claire said. "I've been taking college courses for a year. It's pretty easy."

I smiled uneasily. For the first time, it appeared she might not understand me. She was busy planning a wedding and working towards a future filled with hope and promise. I was a big, fat nothing.

"You have to stop feeling sorry for yourself," Claire said.

"Why? It feels good," I answered.

She draped her arm around my shoulder. It was a move my mother might have made.

"You're eighteen years old and you walk around like you're carrying the weight of the world," she said.

I hated that she was talking down to me. This was all her fault. If she just loved me back, everything would be perfect.

"Remember two things," she said. "First, life gets harder every day."

"That's refreshing," I said.

"Secondly, only you can arrange your life. You'll make your own reality."

It was Claire's way of telling me to get off my ass.

"Can you go with me tomorrow?" I asked.

She looked away, pulling her arm from my shoulder.

"I'm sorry," she said. "I can't."

The feeling of being absolutely alone was almost overwhelming.

"Leo, I'm getting married. I can't keep holding your hand. You need a life, without me as the cornerstone."

Claire was on the verge of tears. I don't think she came over to tell me off, but that's where we were. I did the only thing I could. Like my father, I walked away. By the time I crawled back through my bedroom window, I was dry heaving because of the sobs that shook my body.

My mother shook me awake. The day was sunny and bright and I wished it were raining. I wasn't sure exactly what to wear to visit colleges, but I didn't have to worry - my mother had set my clothes out for me. I kept hearing Claire's voice. She was right; I was pathetic.

My mother, on the other hand, was bristling with excitement. Perhaps it was the fact that I'd be out of the house next year and she'd be free to do Keith in any room she wanted.

"I figure we'll drive to Gannon and hit Fredonia on the way back," she said.

She put scrambled eggs and bacon in front of me.

"Have you given much thought to what you might like to major in?" she asked.

She sipped her coffee and watched me eat.

"Not really," I said.

Her eyes sort of drifted away and I took it that she was daydreaming of my future.

"You like sports," she said. "Maybe you can be a sportswriter or an announcer or something."

It was exactly what Dad had said, and I figured out that they were talking about me when I wasn't around.

"Yeah, maybe," I said.

What if Weird Henry was right? What if I paid all that money to go to school and died before I was ever presented with a diploma?

"Maybe college isn't for me," I said.

My mother reacted as though she'd been slapped.

"I could work at a grocery store or something, and hang around here," I said.

She smiled as if to say that I was completely out of my mind.

"You're too smart for that."

I wasn't sure how she knew that, but I shoveled the last of the eggs into my mouth and returned the smile. It was sweet of her to think so, but what mother ever wanted to face the fact that her son was a loser?

"It's kind of funny," Mom said, "but when you were born, we talked about all the possibilities of what you might become. Your father always said you'd be a successful lawyer, or the president of a corporation."

"I'm pretty disappointing, huh?"

"Of course not," Mom said. "You're going to make a real name for your-self. I still think you're going to be a big star. Some day you'll be on national television and everyone will be waiting to hear what you have to say."

I laughed at her eternal optimism. Given my life up to that point, I really didn't feel like a star.

◊ ◊ ◊

At Gannon University, I stood in line with hundreds of anonymous people. I wondered if everyone was as frightened as me. There was a lot of excited chatter and bursts of laughter, but just as in high school, I was on the outside looking in. I was so involved in my self-loathing that I hardly felt the tap on my right shoulder.

"Where you from?"

A terribly excited, very pretty, slightly overweight girl was standing behind the question.

"Buffalo," I said.

She shrieked in excitement and I nearly fell out of my place in line.

"I go there all the time," she said. "My Dad takes us to football games and it's just a fun city. Isn't it a lot of fun?"

"Like a barrel of monkeys," I said.

She laughed uproariously and slapped me on the back. Again, I damn near lost my footing.

"I'm Michelle. I'm from Erie, and people say I talk a lot but that's all right, right?"

She didn't wait for my answer.

"I can show you the town if you'd like. I'm a sophomore. I know all the good spots."

She elbowed me in the ribs and I stumbled back.

"Would you be interested in that?" she asked.

"That would be wonderful," I said.

She turned away for a second and I nearly started to breathe normally again.

"There's someone I want you to meet," she said.

She scanned the crowd for a sign of her friend and I thought about making a run for it.

59

"There he is! Hey, Luke, come here," she shouted.

A good-looking, clean-cut boy shuffled to us. He looked as cool and confident as Steven, and I liked him instantly.

"Luke's from New Jersey," she said. "He's having a party tonight at his apartment. I hope you can come. What's your name?"

"Leo, but I'm not staying overnight. I have another college to visit on the way home."

Luke extended his hand and I shook it sheepishly.

"Leo, my boy, you are home," he said.

◊ ◊ ◊

Maybe my mother *did* want to get rid of me. She was convinced that the party at Luke's was a great idea.

"We can see Fredonia anytime," she said. "I'm real impressed with this place. Spend the night and see if this is where you want to go."

She leaned in to pluck a piece of lint from my shirt. My mother had changed my shit diapers, wiped snot from my nose, and made sure I never went to bed too hungry or sad. Now, she was standing before me, pleading with me to get out of her life. In a way it was almost like she was revitalized by the opportunity to finally live her life. Michael was a huge success, and I was on my way to college. It was time for her to form a life of her own.

She flipped open her purse and extracted thirty-five dollars.

"The bus fare home is twenty dollars," she said. "The buses leave every three hours. Have a good time, meet some new people, and I'll see you tomorrow."

Mom kissed me on the cheek, but she must have noticed my uneasiness.

"Leo, you have to grow up. I won't be around forever."

First Claire, and now my mother, but I could almost understand how she felt. Michael had made the dean's list and all of my friends appeared to be on the right road. I was sleepwalking through all of it. I felt like crying, but I nodded in agreement. As my father might say, it was time to shit or get off the pot.

"You're responsible for yourself now, Leo. Do the right things."

She kissed me and quickly moved away. I couldn't bear to watch her go, so I scanned the gathering of students in search of Luke and Michelle.

◊ ◊ ◊

Plainly put, Luke's apartment was a shithole. The party was held in a dank, dark basement that smelled of beer and cigarettes. That being said, I had never seen a place more alive. The music was so loud that it was almost impossible to talk normally. There were three kegs of beer flowing at all times, and at least a hundred people stood shoulder-to-shoulder, drinking, smoking and laughing.

For the first hour, Luke filled me in on the best fraternities and the best bars. We saluted one another with glass after glass of draft beer. We talked about sports, how to avoid early classes, and how much easier it was to get girls in college as opposed to high school. We were getting along so well that I opened up and told him all about Claire.

We were seated at the bar, out of direct earshot of the music. We were both smoking cigars and emptying beer glasses.

"She's the absolute best looking girl in the world," I said. "She's smart and funny, and she understands me better than anyone in the world."

"Forget her," Luke said.

"She's marrying my best friend, but I swear to God, I want to make one final stand to keep her from doing it."

"Don't even think about it," Luke said.

"I figure I'll rent a white horse and ride it up to the church. Just as she's about to take his hand, I'll bust through the doors and ride straight to the altar. I'll tell her how much I love her and she'll break down crying and ride off with me."

Luke shook his head in disbelief. He refilled my beer glass, and draped his arm over my right shoulder. With his left hand, he took my chin and directed my eyes towards a long-legged blonde. Without hesitating, he turned my head in the other direction to an unbelievably striking brunette whose ass was pointed in our direction as she bent to tie her shoe.

"I'm only going to tell you this once. Pretty girls are a dime a dozen. You're about to enter college and you don't know one friggen' thing about life."

Luke paused as though he had already said too much, but he forged ahead nonetheless.

"I'm sure Claire's the greatest human to walk the planet, but you don't even know what to compare her to. Life isn't always fair, but here's a dose of what's really happening. She doesn't love you. You'll never be her husband," Luke said.

I watched the burning ash of my cigar fall to the filthy basement floor.

"I don't even know you," Luke said. "But last year, I didn't want to give up my old life, either. Starting over isn't always fun, but sometimes you have to because it isn't what you thought it should be."

I thought of my father walking away from us all those years ago. I thought of Claire pushing me away, and my mother tossing me from the nest. It *was* time to sink or swim and after spending a night drowning my sorrows in beer, I would climb back onshore.

◊ ◊ ◊

The bus was virtually empty. My head was cloudy from the beer, and my heart ached a little. I was heading back to my home of eighteen years. It would never be home again. From here on out, I would be a visitor in my old life. I wasn't sure where I was going or if I'd make it, but Luke was right. Down deep, it hadn't meant a thing.

I leaned my head against the window and watched the bus tires speed along the pavement. I couldn't stop myself from crying over Claire, but I swore it would be the very last time. There wouldn't be a white horse and we wouldn't live happily ever after. That was how it was going to be, and no one cared if I liked it or not.

Out of the corner of my eye I noticed a girl who was about seven, watching me as I cried.

"Look at that man," the girl said. "He's crying."

"Just ignore him," the mother whispered.

Yet, before the girl could turn away, I smiled. Somehow, I would work it out. I don't know why it mattered but I didn't want that girl to see me sad.

Chapter Eight

– The Wedding – Part One – August, 1991

"You may already be a loser."— *Form Letter*

My trip to Gannon lent me a glimmer of hope for the rest of my life. I took my mother's suggestion to a new level by concentrating on my blossoming career as a sportswriter. Each day, I retired to my room with the sports page under my arm, attempting to study writing styles. I sent letters to the editor nearly every day, and I dreamed of having my picture appear under a byline. Unfortunately, the editor didn't feel compelled to print any of my letters. Occasionally, I received a rejection letter, but I remained diligent. Someday, I would be a sportswriter.

It was a strange summer to say the least. Michael was hardly ever around as his budding career as an architect, and his girlfriend, Theresa, monopolized his time. Claire and Steven were busy planning their wedding, and I tried to distance myself from Weird Henry. Since the visit to Gannon, I kept in contact with Luke and Michelle. I needed to establish a life, and since my past was abandoning me, I had nothing to do but look forward. Yet, I couldn't pretend that my heart wasn't broken.

It all started with the engagement announcement. Claire and Steven pronounced their love for one another with a huge photo published in the town newspaper. I clipped the picture and stared at it in the quiet of my room. Her smile was perfect. Their hands were coupled, and Steven's expression appeared to be mocking me. I would spend the rest of my life knowing that he was married to my wife. A couple of things brought a profound sadness bubbling to the surface.

I was working as a stock boy at the local grocery store. I absolutely hated the job, and it wasn't because of the work. I just couldn't stand being on display as I performed one menial task after another. Yet, I needed money for school, and sometimes you have to do what you don't want to do.

I was bagging groceries when Claire and Steven walked through the front door. As usual, my heart jumped when I saw her, but she held his hand tightly as she smiled in my direction. The customers were standing five-deep in my line, and I wasn't sure it was such a good time to be distracted from the task at hand.

"We have to ask you something," she sang.

Steven placed his arm around my right shoulder.

"Will you be our best man?" he asked.

The cashier began ringing up the next customer's gigantic order. The bitter, old woman who had probably planned her entire day around the trip to the grocery store screamed at me to double-bag everything. I offered her my best stock boy smile.

"I wanted you as matron of honor, but I had to choose a female," Claire said. She laughed a bit too loudly and I scanned the front of the store for a sign of my manager.

"It was an easy choice for me, too," Steven said.

They looked so healthy and strong, and so in love, that I had to turn away from them. I tried concentrating on what I was putting into the bags, but everything was coming at me so fast.

"Don't make them too heavy," the old lady shouted. "I have to carry them up a flight of stairs and if one of them breaks, I'll come back looking for you."

I pulled her cart closer and smiled.

"Will you do it?" Claire asked.

She was so close that I could have kissed her without straining.

"Of course; I'd be honored," I said.

Claire *did* kiss me and Steven patted me on the back.

"I told you to watch what you're doing. That bag is too damn heavy," the old lady scowled.

I pulled a couple of cans of tomatoes out of the bag and opened another bag. The groceries were jamming the belt in front of me and the lady was watching me like a hawk.

"The wedding's in three weeks," Claire said.

She was so excited, and I loved her so much that it was impossible not to smile.

"You have to get fitted for a tux, write a toast, and find a date," Steven said.

"I wish you people would leave him alone," the crotchety old bitch called out. "He's obviously not smart enough to pack a bag and talk at the same time."

"I'll come by after my shift," I whispered. "We can have a few beers and talk about it."

"Oh, I can't imagine you drunk," the lady said. There wasn't anything wrong with the old bag's hearing.

Thankfully, the order was nearly complete.

"I *have* a date," I said. "I met a girl at orientation that I really like."

It was a total lie and a truly pathetic, last-ditch effort to make Claire jealous.

"That's great," she said. "You can bring whoever you want. Any friend of yours is a friend of mine."

I searched her face for a hint of jealousy, but it wasn't there. My mind was a whirlwind as I tried to register everything. I broke the cardinal rule of packing by putting a bar of soap on top of a package of pork chops. I caught my own mistake and tossed the soap aside. There was no doubt that I had been seen.

"Why would you pick that dim-wit as best man?" the woman asked.

I caught Claire's sparkling eyes. She winked so quickly that I thought I imagined it.

"I'll pack the rest," she said.

I stepped out of the way and watched Claire deftly place the groceries in the bags. At the very last second, she reached in, grabbed the soap, and tossed it back into the bag with the meat.

"Lighten up lady. Life's too short to be miserable the whole way."

Claire smiled bright as day, and the lady hid her eyes.

◊ ◊ ◊

When my shift was over, I returned to an empty house. There was a note from my mother attached to a chicken potpie. She was out with Keith again. I tossed the potpie into the garbage and rummaged through the mail. It was a big day for me. I read a welcoming letter from Gannon, ignored what I imagined was a story rejection from the *Buffalo News*, and slipped into a sitting position, holding the wedding invitation.

My eyes filled with tears, as I ran my finger along the edge of the envelope. Their names were emblazoned in gold. I closed my eyes and imagined that my name was listed under Claire's. That's how it should've been. I'm not sure how long I held the invitation to my face, but it was at least ten minutes. I had no idea what it felt like to be catatonic, but I was close.

Finally, seeing enough, I tossed the invitation in the direction of the potpie. I grabbed a beer and, looking for even more misery, picked up the letter from the paper. In my mind, I went over the contents of my suicide note. It had been cool for Romeo and Juliet to kill themselves in an expression of love. Why wouldn't it be cool for me?

It wasn't the standard rejection letter. In fact, the correspondence was directly from the desk of the head sports editor, Larry Anderson. It was a quick, handwritten note that said, "Call me — I have an internship for the summer."

I slugged the beer down and pressed my eyes closed. There was a chance that I was imaging the words on the paper. When I opened my eyes, they were still there. I emitted a short, almost girlish yelp, and was ashamed for having contemplated suicide. I was on my way to the big time! I grabbed two more beers and skipped out the front door.

I didn't even stop to knock on Claire's front door. This was the biggest news of my life and I had to share it with her.

Claire and Steven were together on the love seat, poring over a bridal magazine. I shared the letter with them and we hugged one another for all that we were worth. It was as though I had already won the Pulitzer Prize. It was then that Claire said the words that stayed with me for years to come.

"When your heart aches from the things your head imagines, don't despair; the world will take care of you."

◊ ◊ ◊

It was two in the morning when my mother returned from her date. I was on the couch with the wedding invitation, the internship offer, and seven empty beer cans.

"What are you doing?" Mom asked.

She looked absolutely radiant. After all the years and all the pain of divorce, she was still a beautiful woman. Maybe that's what life is all about. You're force-fed mountains of shit, and you have to battle your way through it.

I handed her the letter and the invitation and sat back, awaiting her reaction. She read them both and got up quickly. She returned with two beers, and popped the tabs.

"In celebration and commiseration," she said.

I hoisted the beer and tapped her can.

"I doubt if it's a paid internship," I said.

"We'll make it work. Your father will have to kick in."

I sipped the beer.

"Claire and Steven asked me to be best man," I said.

"You *are* the best man," she said, but her face showed a hint of worry. "They remind me of your father and me. We were so young and stupid. We thought that love would conquer all. We never considered that the love might fade, and we weren't ready to handle it when it did."

"Love sucks," I said.

She just smiled. She gulped her beer and put her arm around my shoulder. I caught the scent of her perfume and for the first time, I realized Keith was lucky to have her.

"Sometimes I feel bad about the way things worked out for you boys," Mom said.

"You shouldn't," I said.

"When I was your age, I imagined life from start to finish."

She looked profoundly saddened by the course of her life, and I realized there was a certain degree of regret that just comes with living.

"I didn't even consider divorce," she said. "Things get screwed-up."

"I'll find another Claire, won't I?" I asked.

"Someday, you'll struggle to remember what she even looked like."

I had no idea how that could ever be true, but I trusted my mother. I hugged her tightly. For a solitary moment, I felt as though I were a baby in her arms again.

◊ ◊ ◊

Three weeks later, Claire and Steven became husband and wife. I stood beside them as a witness of their love and commitment. Deep in my heart, I was happy for them. They belonged together. We would continue to grow as friends. What choice did I have? Oh yeah, and Claire was the most beautiful bride you'll ever see.

Chapter Nine

– Headed for a fall – January, 1993

"It is better to know some of the questions than all of the answers."
—James Thurber

My relationship with my father had completely deteriorated, but from time to time, I caught myself thinking about some of the things he'd told me. One of his all-time favorite sayings was that all through life, you'd look behind you, wondering what the hell you were thinking. I entered my third year of college doing just that. From what I could see, Claire and Steven had settled nicely into their marriage. Claire finished college in record time and was working as a professor's assistant at the University at Buffalo. She was studying for her master's degree and earning money. Steven graduated early from Canisius College and took a job as an accountant, making over twenty thousand dollars a year. They were set. I was in trouble.

It wasn't that I didn't enjoy college. I understood that I had to have the degree in hand before I could score big with the *Buffalo News*. The problem was I had already been inside the newsroom. I understood what it took to get through the day, and the studying bored me. I spent the first couple of years trying to drink Erie dry. While I knew all I needed to know, I couldn't pass the tests because I couldn't make the classes, and I couldn't make the classes because I couldn't get out of bed. It was a vicious cycle.

As I neared mid-semester break, it was becoming painfully apparent that some changes would have to be made. I was taking a class called "Broadcast Television" and while it should have been easy, I was on the verge of failure. My professor was an uninteresting man named Ed

O'Banick and the reason why I was in his class was because I heard he grad-ed leniently. The students used to say, "Don't panic, take O'Banick."

In my case, it wasn't working. I'll never forget the class because it was a turning point in my life. O'Banick had an irritating habit of involving the entire class in his discussions. Since I usually had a swollen head from par-tying the night before, I never felt quite like participating. O'Banick knew this.

"All right, we're talking about Charlie Chaplin and the influence of the silent film era on the early days of television. Can someone explain this influence to me?" O'Banick asked.

I bowed my head and covered my eyes with my right hand. Somehow, I knew he was looking at me.

"Mr. Brown, do you have any ideas?"

"Not one," I said.

The class laughed a bit too loudly.

"What do you know about Chaplin?" he asked.

He edged closer to my seat in the back row. More than anything else, I was afraid of total embarrassment.

"He was a deaf mute," I said.

There was more muffled laughter, but O'Banick didn't back down.

"Tell me about the early days of television," he said.

"Jack Benny, George Burns, Bob Hope, wasn't it?" I asked.

O'Banick was actually grinding his teeth. Not many people know this, but it is difficult to be evicted from a college class. The professor would rather hand out a failing grade than risk the wrath of being seen as some-one who did not treat the paying student fairly. I understood that O'Banick would glare at me and then move on. But he didn't.

"Get the hell out of here," he said.

The class went silent. I couldn't believe he was serious. My parents were paying good money for my education. Who the hell did he think he was? I didn't make a move.

"I said, get out!" O'Banick screamed.

I took my time gathering up my books and he actually had the gall to stand just inches from me. If I didn't know better, I would've thought he might hit me.

"I don't have time to waste on you," he said. "You won't amount to anything more than a huge pile of shit."

"At least I'll be a huge one," I said.

The class erupted into laughter once more as I shuffled out the door, humiliated in every way.

That night, I replayed the event over and over in my mind. It would be so much easier just to quit school and start work at a newspaper. But who would hire me?

I struggled out of bed and searched my room for the faculty directory. O'Banick's name was listed in the theater arts section. Beside his office address, he listed his home telephone number. I stared at that number until it was etched upon my brain and I imagined a hundred different conversations. In the most courageous move of my life, I punched the numbers into the telephone and waited through four extremely long rings.

I recognized O'Banick's tired voice. I nearly lost my nerve and slammed down the phone, but at the last moment, I recited my name.

"I'm glad you called," O'Banick said. "I was afraid you were a lost cause."

He agreed to meet me at a little diner on the edge of campus. I arrived first, and slugged down a cup of coffee as I waited for him. O'Banick stepped through the doors and scanned the nearly empty place for a sign of me. In a strange sort of way, he looked a lot like my father. His hair was thinning, and his gut hung way over his belt. He actually smiled, and all at once, it hit me. This was a man who obviously cared. Students took his class for a chance at an easy grade, but he didn't just hand them out. I didn't know the man, but in the middle of the night, he had come to save me.

He extended his right hand and I shook it.

"Best handful of shit I've had all day," he said.

I started to laugh, but midway through it, I was near tears.

"I don't know what I'm doing," I said. "My mother's breaking her ass for me to get an education and I'm screwing it up."

O'Banick edged into the booth next to me and I couldn't even begin to think how strange we looked sitting side-by-side.

"It isn't too late," he said. "A lot of people make mistakes in life, but don't realize it until they're so far lost they can't ever get back."

"I know I can be a sports reporter," I said.

"There's no doubt about it," he answered.

O'Banick sat beside me for a few more minutes, and when he was sure that I was through blubbering, he moved across from me.

"I need to tell you a story," he said.

The waitress interrupted us for a moment.

"Can I help you?" she asked.

She was a mildly attractive woman, but I wouldn't have given her more than a split-second glance. O'Banick smiled at her as if had known her all his life. He leaned close to read her nametag.

"How are you tonight, Debbie?"

"Fine," she said.

"That's good. A cup of coffee, and I'll try the apple pie," O'Banick said.

She shifted her gaze to me.

"Just coffee," I said.

I was afraid to admit that on my college budget I couldn't afford to eat. O'Banick must have sensed my problem. Debbie was nearly back to her station before O'Banick called to her.

"Say, Debbie, could you make that two slices of pie?"

She nodded and smiled.

"About ten years ago, Gannon had the best baseball team in division two."

I felt ashamed for nearly crying.

"The best player on the team was a slugger named Tony Martin. God, he had it all. He hit for power, threw the ball a hundred miles an hour, and ran like a deer."

O'Banick had a twinkle in his eye as he imagined watching Tony Martin play ball.

"He was also as dumb as a rock," he said.

The waitress returned to the table and O'Banick put about seven teaspoons of sugar into his coffee.

"Of course, Tony took a couple of classes from me. You know, 'don't panic, take O'Banick'."

I acted surprised, but O'Banick waved me off.

"I've heard it all," he said. "Anyway, I couldn't pass him. He didn't do any of the work. He was an absolute nightmare in the classroom, and he

72

didn't heed the warnings. About halfway through the year, I told him exactly what I'm telling you."

I darted my eyes away, almost ashamed to hear it.

"I told Martin he was headed for a big fall off a short cliff."

I didn't dare look up. Honestly, I didn't want to hear the rest of the story.

"I also told him he was in danger of failing my class. He was shocked. I'm O'Banick. No one fails my class."

I had to stifle a laugh. It was exactly what I was thinking.

"The next day, Tony dropped out of my class. He evidently didn't find many teachers who wanted to push him through. When his athletic eligibility was up, he needed thirty credits to graduate," O'Banick said.

Thirty credits amounted to just about a full year.

"What happened to him?" I asked.

"Just what I expected. He fell real fast."

O'Banick stopped long enough to get his pie from the waitress. He also sighed heavily. I could tell he was battling the rest of the story. I knew that the ending probably wasn't good.

"He was drafted by the Expos in the very last round. For awhile, we pretended that he might make it someday."

I concentrated on the apple pie for a moment.

"Two years into minor league ball in Vancouver, Tony broke his leg in about six places. He got tangled up with the first baseman, and for awhile it was touch and go on whether or not he'd keep the leg."

O'Banick wiped his eyes with his napkin. Everything about the man was pretty much exactly opposite of my former perception of him.

"Sports stars get injured," I said.

"All of the promise was gone," O'Banick said. "The doctors fixed up his leg and about three months after he could walk again, Tony strolled in front of a Greyhound bus bound for Alberta."

I all but dropped my fork.

"The driver said he just stood there and took it."

I don't know what came over me, but I actually felt like laughing. It was all so ridiculous. Weird Henry's father had shot his own head off, and Tony Martin walked in front of a bus.

"I'm not about to walk in front of a bus," I said.

73

O'Banick took a huge piece of pie and I watched as it dangled on the edge of his fork.

"Maybe not literally," he said.

He chewed the pie for what seemed like twenty minutes and he chased it with a gulp of coffee.

"Leo, no one will hand you a single thing. You might have it all mapped out right now, but if you don't work, you won't make it. That's the story of life. You can only take out what you've already put in."

I don't remember us parting that night. In fact, I'm not even sure another word passed between us, although there must have been something. I passed O'Banick's class with flying colors and my grade point average improved almost a full point after our conversation.

One day soon after, I leafed through an old Gannon prospectus from the days when Tony Martin ruled the baseball team. He had a career batting average of close to four hundred. He hit thirty-six home runs in one year, which was still a school record. Under a photo of Tony Martin, his date of birth and date of death were listed. The most important statistic of all was that he had lived exactly *one* failed life. Tony Martin never saw his twenty-third birthday. He never graduated from college, and he didn't play for the Yankees. It was the most important lesson I ever learned in college and it came from the easiest touch on campus.

Chapter Ten

– The Miseducation of Leo Brown – January, 1995

"Reality is a crutch for people who can't cope with drugs."
—Lily Tomlin

A couple of very important things happened during my senior year at Gannon. First and foremost, I secured a real job. Secondly, life's lessons continued to crash directly into my mid-section.

I was hired as an assistant to the editor of the daily news at WCNE-TV in Erie. My dream job, of course, would have been the sports editor of the Erie newspaper, but at least I was working in my field of study. Since the run-in with O'Banick, things had smoothed out and I was well on the way to graduating. I was happy with myself for the first time in a long time.

I arrived at WCNE well before my shift was to start. I was ready for the chaos, but it was much more than I imagined.

I was ushered into Angelo Martinez's office. Martinez was the number one newshound in Erie. I remember thinking I should treasure the fact that I was shaking his hand, but the handshake never came. Martinez was buried behind an avalanche of paperwork, and he didn't have time for pleasantries.

"Sit down," he said.

He pointed to a chair that was over-run with old newspapers. I debated setting the papers on the floor, but when I gauged his impatience, I simply sat on top of the pile.

"You're supposed to be good, right?" he asked.

I didn't know how to answer the question, so I nodded.

"As you can see, I'm buried up to my ass here. It's about time I got help."

He was so much different from his on-screen personality, I couldn't help but stare. When Angelo Martinez delivered the news, the people of Erie sat up and listened. Behind the eleven o'clock news desk, he was handsome, charismatic, and chock full of wisdom. Sitting in the chair in his unbelievably disorganized office, he looked like a homeless man.

"I need help with copies, typing and fucking filing."

He tossed papers into the air. I had actually thought he'd help me form a career as a reporter, but it was looking like he needed a secretary.

"If you're going to learn anything here, you'll learn it on the run. I ain't got time to wipe my ass."

Again, I nodded and battled the approaching laughter.

"You'll get four-seventy an hour. There's no such thing as overtime, either."

Martinez was waiting for me to say something, but the cupboard was bare.

"You graduate in May, right?" he asked.

I answered with another nod.

"Do you have any questions?" he asked.

"How's the four-seventy an hour figured?"

He looked as if I'd stumped him somehow. He pushed a pile of papers to one side and picked up half an egg sandwich that must have been left from the day before.

"It's fucking minimum wage," he said.

He laughed through three bites of the sandwich.

We stepped through the main lobby and descended the stairs at a furious pace. I carried a file box of papers and Angelo was in front of me, turning on lights and kicking shit down the stairs.

"Where are we going?" I asked.

"I work better away from everyone else," Angelo said.

He flicked on an overhead light and a must-covered, leaking basement came into view. The basement was home to hundreds of file cabinets.

"This is the records room," Angelo said. "I keep an office here so I can get away from the fucking noise."

Sure enough, tucked back between the files was a small desk with a portable typewriter. A sign posted above the desk proclaimed "WCNE...Erie's CNN."

Angelo caught me looking at the sign.

"Yeah, we're CNN all right. Hey, are you cool or not?"

It was another unanswerable question.

Angelo sat behind the typewriter. He opened the bottom desk drawer and pulled out a paper lunch bag. He appeared to be waiting for an answer.

"Am I cool?" I asked.

He handed me the bag.

"Open it. I need to see your reaction."

I did as I was told, and I immediately recognized the contents as cocaine. In my distorted little world, I imagined Angelo had come across it while doing a story on the drug traffic in Erie.

"What're you going to do with it?" I asked. I was trying to appear cool.

Angelo started laughing. "I'm going to fucking snort it. What do you think?"

So, there I was. On the morning of my first real job, I was sequestered in the basement of the newsroom watching one of my idols snort cocaine as though he were a common addict.

"It's the only way I make it through the day," he said.

That night, I watched Angelo Martinez report on a story about corruption at City Hall. His performance was flawless.

◊ ◊ ◊

My run-in with Martinez left me feeling disillusioned. I returned to the apartment I shared with Luke and Gretchen with my mind on a couple of beers. The apartment was empty and there was a note explaining they had gone to the library.

I crumpled the note and stared at the telephone. I considered calling Claire for some sort of advice, but any way you sliced it, she wouldn't be interested. Of course, she'd act like it was important to her, but we both knew it wasn't.

I hit the message button on the blinking answering machine and Weird Henry's voice filled the room. "Leo, my man, Weird Henry here.

What's going on? I hope you're finally getting some down there. I was just having a couple of beers. I've had a rough stretch of it lately, but you know me. Anyway, do good, college boy. I'll be watching you."

I wasn't exactly sure what Weird Henry was trying to say, and it really didn't matter. I had problems of my own. I couldn't figure out why I was so down. Was it because I thought life would be different in the real world? Had I imagined that grown-up professionals would act like adults? I decided to go to a bar to have a couple of beers to clear my head.

I entered the *Shaggy Dog* saloon at six-thirty. There was just one other patron in the bar, and to my amazement, she knew me. She spoiled my desire to be alone by sitting beside me.

Amy Moran's eyes were as blue as the sea. Her auburn hair hung to her shoulders and a pair of the world's tightest blue jeans outlined her slim body. She was a beautiful girl in every manner of speaking, but she wasn't exactly the most popular girl on campus. She knew it, and didn't care.

"Bad, bad Leo Brown," she said.

She was on a lonely bar run of her own, and it had started quite some time ago.

"That's Leroy Brown," I said.

She winked and smiled.

"Not tonight it isn't."

Amy was the prettiest girl that had ever shown an interest in me, but I wasn't smart enough to realize that she was considering me as a potential boyfriend.

"You seem a little sad," she said.

"I don't know what it is," I said. "There's like a void in my heart that I can't seem to fill. I went to work with Angelo Martinez today."

"Wow, that's great," she said.

"He wasn't what I expected him to be," I said.

She sort of half-smiled as though I were absolutely pitiful.

"You're cute," she said.

I almost looked behind me to see whom she was talking about. I pointed to the center of my chest and rolled my eyes.

"Yes, you," she said. "Don't sell yourself short."

I ordered two more beers.

"The thing is, you can't expect too much of people. We all have our faults."

I thought of Claire and how she seemed to be perfection personified.

"What's paradise to you?" Amy asked.

She pushed her empty bottle across the bar and immediately grabbed the full one. I shrugged.

"Can I take a stab at what you're all about?"

"Be my guest," I said. I laughed at our little game, but she seemed to be all business.

"You're carrying a torch for some girl from back home, right?" Amy said. She batted her eyelashes and giggled in a truly wonderful manner.

"You want a woman that you can adore forever. I'm figuring you for a couple of kids, two cars in the garage and a mansion on a hill."

"Sort of," I said. I couldn't help but think of Weird Henry's assessment of my life ten years down the road.

"Then she'll walk away from you and you'll be stuck living in a tiny apartment somewhere, wondering how you'll pay the child support."

Amy was in a full-fledged laughing fit. I was stuck between laughter and wondering how she could say such a miserable thing.

"That's awful," I said.

"You're a nice guy," she said. "Sooner or later, you'll get everything you want, but if you expect perfection, you'll end up hurting."

I was instantly sold on her. We sat in silence for a moment, and while I debated kissing her, she leaned in close and took control. Our kiss lasted for nearly a full minute, and outside of the moment when my lips met Claire's, it was the best kiss in the world.

"Life is about fighting to pay the bills," she said. "You'll go to your kid's football games and drink a few beers on the weekend. Maybe you'll need to escape the reality of it all for awhile, who knows?"

She flicked her wonderful hair away from her face. She took a healthy pull from her beer and placed her hand on my thigh.

"Collectively, we don't know jack-shit about living the right way. We chase one thing after another, believing when we finally have it, we've made it."

Angelo Martinez had it all, but for some reason, he had to get coked out of his brain to live the right way. Part of my brain wanted to get away from being so cynical about it, but I was powerless to resist such a gorgeous messenger.

"So, what do you suggest?" I asked.

"Wallow in the pity," she said. "That's what we all end up doing, anyway."

We had three more beers and with our inhibitions clearly blown away, we decided to continue the party back at my place. We skipped out of the *Shaggy Dog* holding hands and I actually believed I could get beyond the sadness I felt earlier. Once again, I was mistaken.

◊ ◊ ◊

When I opened the front door, my heart actually skipped a beat. Claire sat on the couch flanked by Steven and my brother, Michael. Her eyes immediately went to Amy and I searched those eyes for a glint of jealousy. It wasn't there.

"Hey, what's up?" I asked.

I was genuinely excited by the prospect of being with everyone, but they were all looking at me kind of strange.

"We've got some news," Michael said.

I glanced at Luke and Gretchen. They wouldn't even look at me.

"What is it?" I asked.

Amy broke away and headed to the kitchen for a beer. Claire immediately came to be by my side.

"Weird Henry died today," Michael said.

I felt as though my legs had been cut out from under me. I stumbled back towards the door, but Claire's hand steadied me.

"He was busted for possession a couple of days ago, and yesterday he was fired from his job."

"But how'd he die?" I asked.

I thought of the message on the answering machine, and I knew how it happened before Michael actually said the words.

"He shot himself," Michael said. "His mother found him sitting in a chair in their living room."

I tried to imagine it. I covered my eyes with my hands and actually tried to hear the gunshot. How could he do such a thing? I pictured that

80

chair of death, and my heart felt as if it might explode. The tears fell from my eyes as though there was something broken inside of me.

Amy came skipping out of the kitchen with two more beers. She attempted to hand one to me, but I pushed her hand away.

"What's going on?" she asked.

I just didn't want to be around it anymore. I slammed out the front door and ran down the street. I didn't have an idea where I was heading and I was at least three blocks away from the apartment before I figured out that it was raining.

◊ ◊ ◊

I entered the darkened apartment a little before four. The effects of the beer had worn thin and I had a bit of a headache. Claire and Steven were asleep on the couch, and Michael was at their feet on the floor. I knew I had driven them crazy with worry, but I still didn't feel much like talking. I shuffled up to my bedroom with thoughts of Weird Henry battering my brain.

I lay in bed tossing my childhood back and forth through my mind. I clearly saw Weird Henry's face, with the perpetual cigarette sticking out of the left corner of his mouth. *He was actually dead.*

The tears came all at once. For some reason, I thought of Archie, my dog that had gotten hit by a car. In some ways, Weird Henry was also struck and killed.

There was a soft knock on the door and I didn't have to be a genius to figure out who was on the other side.

Claire entered slowly. She sat on the edge of the bed. She pulled my head up to her bosom.

"You live and you love. You love and you lose," she said. "That's all I can tell you."

She kissed my forehead as though I were a child. Weird Henry was gone and Claire was with me to pick up the pieces.

"I don't know how to live," I said.

"We'll get through it together," Claire answered. She caressed my cheek as if I were a newborn child.

"Everything I thought I knew is just shit," I cried.

81

"You'll find a reason to believe again," Claire said. "I'll help you find the reason."

Two days later, I received the letter. Immediately, I recognized Weird Henry's shaky penmanship. The letter was direct.

"Leo, my man, Keep the faith. Whatever you desire will be yours. I just had to escape. Sorry. Weird Henry."

Chapter Eleven

– Graduation – March, 1995

"I don't deserve this award, but I have arthritis and I don't deserve that either." —Jack Benny

Three weeks before graduation, Luke and Gretchen joined us for an evening of binge drinking. About halfway through the night, Luke cornered me in the kitchen.

"How's the job?" he asked.

"Sucks," I said.

"Are you thinking of staying in Erie or going back to Buffalo?"

I still didn't have a clue. As much as I would have liked to go back to my old life, it really wasn't there for me.

"I could stay, I guess," I said, "but Claire and Steven are back in Buffalo."

Luke was tired of my dreaming about Claire. Usually, he tolerated my fantasies, but tonight there was a different sort of look in his eyes.

"You've got to forget Claire," he said. "Amy loves you, man."

I turned away. Could it be true? Did Amy truly love me as a wife loves a husband?

"She doesn't love me," I said.

"Sure she does," Luke said.

He jumped into a sitting position on the kitchen counter and I tossed him another beer.

"In fact, she's thinking of going to Connecticut with us after the ceremony. The only thing holding her here is you."

I still couldn't believe she actually wanted me around. As far as I was concerned, it wasn't anything more than a college crush.

"We eat together, drink together, and sleep together — that's it," I said.

Luke laughed at my sense of logic.

"What else is there?" he asked.

I didn't know how to explain it to him. How do you tell your best college buddy that you're looking for more passion, more sensitivity, more love?

"She doesn't make me feel all giddy inside," I said.

Luke shook his head in pity.

"In fact, sometimes she drives me crazy."

"They'll all drive you crazy," he said.

The beer was clouding my vision of the world, but Luke had a point. It was time to make a major change in my life.

"The way I figure it, you can stay stagnant here, or you can go backwards after Claire."

"My third option?" I asked.

"We can all move forward together. I say we get a place in New Haven. Hell, you'll find a job in a minute. You got a steady girl and we can party on the weekends."

I was peeling my beer label. I was afraid to look up.

"It's still Claire, isn't it?"

I half-nodded.

"God Almighty, she's been married for four freaking years. She isn't coming back for you."

"I know." I said, "I'm just looking for someone who makes me feel like she does."

Luke jumped down from the counter.

"What color is the sky in your world?" Luke asked.

I shrugged his question away.

"Amy's a perfectly good girl."

"I know," I said.

"You ain't going to find one that pukes ice cream."

I started laughing, but I honestly wanted to tell Luke that there was no harm in looking.

"Just think about coming, huh?"

"I will."

◊ ◊ ◊

Of course, Claire was there on graduation day. She made the trip with my mother and Keith. Steven and Michael were playing golf in a corporate tournament, and Dad and Margaret couldn't be bothered. I didn't invite Amy to our little gathering, and it was all just one more attempt to be with Claire. Without Steven and Amy there, I could fantasize that she was mine.

We met for breakfast at *Pete's Diner* on Myrtle Avenue. The diner was empty and Pete stood behind the counter as we shouted our order to him. It was a curious place to celebrate graduation, but it felt right to me.

"I put two kids through college," Mom said proudly.

Yet, it seemed like she was finished with me. She discarded the egg whites and dabbed at the yoke with a piece of dry toast. It was a move that I'd seen her make a thousand times, but that morning, I concentrated on all her movements. Deep down I knew that she was proud of me and that she considered her job complete.

"Keith's company is transferring him to San Jose," she said.

He smiled, but I envisioned him on top of my mother on the living room couch. There was gray hair at his temples. He was dressed fabulously in an expensive suit. I knew it had to be killing him to be sitting in such a restaurant. Still, I wondered what he was all about. Did he really love my mother?

"I'm going with him," Mom said.

I dropped my fork. She was done with me.

"Isn't it wonderful?" Claire asked.

But it wasn't wonderful. It sucked.

"Why don't you come with us for a couple of weeks?" Keith asked.

It was then that I made my decision. Whether I liked it or not, I had to appear that I had some direction.

"Actually, I'm moving too," I said. "I'm going with Luke, Gretchen, and Amy to New Haven, Connecticut."

This time, Claire dropped her fork.

"I have an inside track on a job at the *New Haven Chronicle* and I have to take the chance."

Clifford Fazzolari

Actually, I wasn't even sure if that was the name of the newspaper, but they seemed to believe me. Worry creased my mother's forehead.

"So, you're going to live with this Amy girl?"

She crinkled up her nose as if she weren't living in sin herself. I wanted to stand up to the question. I wanted to make Claire squirm, and more than anything else, I wanted to appear to be a grown-up. I thought of my argument with my father. He dared me to be a man. This was my chance to show all of them.

"We're all going as roommates," I said. "It's no big deal."

My mother turned her attention back to her egg. I had distracted her for all of five minutes.

"I have a card for you, from all of us," Keith said.

He handed it across the table. I considered it for a second and then placed it beside my plate.

"Maybe you should open it," Mom said.

It was your standard card of congratulations, but the ten, one-hundred-dollar bills that fluttered to the table were not standard by any means.

"Holy shit," I said.

"You did a great job," Mom said.

What could I do? I hugged them for all that I was worth.

◊ ◊ ◊

Twenty minutes before my name was called, I slugged from a bottle of bourbon. I had a college degree, a thousand bucks in my pocket, and two beautiful girls beside me.

"I don't know how you can drink that," Claire said.

"It's an acquired taste," Amy said as she grabbed the bottle from my hand.

Claire draped an arm around my shoulder. She took the bottle from Amy.

"For the past twenty-two years I've had to take care of this boy."

She sniffed the bourbon and tossed her head back in horror.

"Today, I'm passing the baton to Amy."

Claire raised the bottle in a toast. She grimaced as she brought it to her lovely lips.

86

"Here's mud in your eye," she said.

I'm not even sure if the bourbon got past her tongue. She started to retch and gag, and she relieved herself of her breakfast — all over my dress shoes.

As I scampered across the stage with Claire's vomit on me, I couldn't help but think that she hadn't puked ice cream. The Bishop handed me my diploma. If he smelled the alcohol, he didn't let on.

◊ ◊ ◊

That night, we all went to the *Anchor Bar* for a few drinks. I sat flanked by Amy and Claire as we discussed my life up to that point. Of course, I dreaded the future. Mom and Keith were headed to California. Claire was going back to Steven. Michael was a successful architect. Dad didn't have anything to say to me anymore, and of course, he had Margaret.

One by one, they left the bar. Luke and Gretchen headed back to the apartment. My entire life up to that point seemed to walk right out that door. I sat beside Amy. Over and over in my mind, I thought of the fact that Weird Henry was dead.

Amy held my hand and kissed my neck. Every time the front door opened, I hoped it was someone that could yank me back to the past.

"We'll have a great time together," Amy said.

"Without a doubt," I said.

But why did I feel like crying?

Chapter Twelve

– Conception – August, 1995

"Boy meets girl; girl gets boy into pickle; boy gets pickle into girl."
— *Jack Woodford*

The death of Weird Henry weighed on my mind. Night after night, I had the same dream. In the dream, Weird Henry, as real as life, was seated in the suicide chair, saying, *"Keep the faith"*. Across the room, my father sat on the sofa, saying, *"Be a man"*. Each night, I sat bolt upright in bed and battled my own sensibilities.

It took quite awhile for Amy, Luke, Gretchen and I to get settled in Connecticut. I was in a familiar position — totally out-of-place. We found a two-bedroom apartment in West Haven and took to playing house. It should have been an incredible start to a new, exciting life. Luke, Gretchen, and Amy looked at it that way. I was only along for the ride.

I scanned the papers, believing I deserved a dream job. I applied for positions that required ten years of experience. When I interviewed, I asked for two grand more than what my potential boss was making. After three weeks, I had a fistful of rejections, and my ever-present aching heart.

The job I finally accepted was for a magazine, *World Events*, that on the brink of bankruptcy. Miserable doesn't even to begin to describe the experience.

Amy was flourishing. She took a job at a retail store in the mall, and within three months was promoted to assistant general manager. She was also totally in love with me, which was absolutely maddening.

Every night that summer, we took long walks along the shore of the Long Island Sound. We'd hold hands, smile a lot, and eat ice cream cones. We had the water, the sun, total freedom, enough money to make it through, and mutual respect and admiration. Through it all, I never really stopped to think that we were forming a life. On one such walk, in the middle of the summer of '95, we approached the heart of the matter.

"Do you have regrets in life?" Amy asked.

I felt her hand, warm in my own.

"Besides Claire, I mean," she teased.

There had never been a reason to deny my true feelings. Amy accepted Claire's existence as a minor annoyance. Everyone was so sure that I'd eventually battle my way through it.

"You know, now that you ask, my relationship with my Dad is a real downer. I have such a hard time working it out in my mind. I mean, he's hardly talked to me in five years."

It was something I had never actually said aloud, but I doubt if Amy was surprised. We walked down a long pier and settled in at the edge of the dock. It was a familiar spot, and I was almost comfortable.

"When I think about it, it drives me crazy," I said. "He had two kids and a good woman, and he walked away from us. He never really came back, you know? Then he tells me I should learn how to be a man."

"I'm not a psychiatrist, but I know how that might make you feel," Amy said.

She gently rubbed my right leg, her hand moving up and down my thigh.

"It's hard to accept," I said. "It's almost like he got to that point in his life, took stock of everything, and decided that wasn't what he wanted. He didn't want Michael, Mom, or me anymore."

"Maybe you're over-simplifying it," she said.

It was at that point that it dawned on me. I was doing exactly what he'd done. I was going through the motions with Amy, just as my father had done with Mom. I broke free of Amy, and struggled to find my feet. I pictured a time down the road when I'd wake up and struggle with the idea of getting out. I didn't consider my relationship with Amy. Instead, I became overwhelmed with the idea that I'd walk away from her someday.

"What's wrong?" Amy asked.

She stood before me as a beautiful, vibrant woman. She was intelligent, happy, and perfectly suited to me in every way. She was my mother in the equation of my father's life. I realized that unless I changed my way of thinking, I would eventually ruin her life.

"What did I say?" she asked.

Her face was a picture of fear and pain.

"What are we doing?" I asked.

She was on the verge of tears, and she didn't even know why. She moved towards me, and I stepped back. Her eyes shifted to a look of horror.

"Leo, what is it?"

"We're at a crossroads," I said.

"What the hell are you talking about?" Her voice shrieked as though I'd hit her.

"Am I going to be my father in ten years?"

The reality of it crashed down on her. She was thinking right along with me, and it crushed her.

"You don't love me?" she asked.

I looked at the miles of water. Of course I loved her, but would I love her forever? I couldn't answer her.

"You son-of-a-bitch," she said.

I wanted to go to her, but something made me stay away.

"I didn't say I don't love you," I said.

Amy turned from me.

"You didn't have to," she said. She sat at the edge of the dock. "But, you can add this to the equation. I missed my fucking period."

A wave of sheer terror enveloped me. It was as if someone had poured hot tar down my throat. I found myself moving towards her. Sobs rocked her body, but when I touched her, she screamed. I turned to the beach, wondering who might be watching. I felt like I was watching the scene from afar, as though it was a movie that was neither funny nor exciting, but just plain sad. What came out of my mouth was totally ignorant. It was something my father might have said.

"How'd that happen?" I asked.

She was up on her feet.

"How'd it happen? How the fuck did it happen? Sex, you dumb bastard."

She was on top of me in a matter of seconds. She slapped at me wildly, catching me flush on the side of my head. I put my hands up to defend myself, but I couldn't stop her. She led me to the very edge of the dock. We both knew that she could've pushed me into the water. I glanced down at my feet. I was completely out of room.

"I'm the dumb bastard," she said. "I pretended we had a life together."

I attempted to wrap my arms around her, and it was all the prompting she needed. She shoved me backwards and I spun around in midair. Just before I hit the water, a tremendous feeling of joy overtook me. *I was going to be a father.*

Amy ran down the beach. I pictured Weird Henry in my mind. From somewhere out there, he was laughing at me. The words of his suicide note echoed through my mind. *"Leo, my man, keep the faith. Whatever you desire will be yours. I just had to escape. Sorry. Weird Henry."*

◊ ◊ ◊

I caught up with Amy about a half-mile down the beach. I wouldn't have if she hadn't wanted me to.

"I do love you," I kept saying over and over. The water was inching its way down my face and I kept combing my hair with my hand. "We'll make it work."

Claire's name kept popping into my head, but I fought it for all I was worth. This was about personal responsibility. This was about a real, living person. It was about my son or daughter growing inside of Amy. It was the story of my life, shoved directly down my throat.

She let me hold her then. She trembled like a bird and every sob tore at my insides. I stroked her hair, whispering that it would be all right. I wanted to cry right along with her, but I held it in.

"We'll do it right," I said.

"It doesn't work without love," she said.

What was happening around us didn't matter. A middle-aged couple with a small, black dog on a leash passed by, but I would have missed them had the dog not barked.

"Is everything all right?" the man asked.

Amy wiped at her tears.

"We're fine," I said.

The man and woman went on their merry way.

"Are we fine?" Amy asked.

The fading sun dried me just enough to make me shiver.

"You didn't have to push me in the lake," I said.

"Yeah, I did," she said. She was half-laughing and half-crying.

It was the defining moment of my life. Up to that point, I had been trapped in a world of illusion. Once again, I was reminded that there truly wasn't a Santa Claus.

"We'll go to the doctor's together," I said. "Whatever happens, we'll handle it."

Amy studied my face. She searched for the slightest trace of apprehension.

"We can abort all of this," she said. "We can end the baby's life and our relationship all in one fell swoop."

She was crying again, and this time, I joined her.

"You asked me if I had any regrets," I said.

I let the statement hang in the air as I tried to gather myself enough to say the right thing.

"If we abort any of this, my life will be a litany of regret."

Amy fell into my arms. We were still crying, but at least we were doing it together. The thought of Claire be damned. For the first time, I saw it for what it was worth. My love for Claire was an adolescent dream. It was my escape route. It was my father running away. It was Weird Henry committing suicide. Yet, even if they couldn't live their lives right, what was stopping me from doing the right thing?

I kissed her forehead lightly. She looked at me and I saw the beginnings of a smile in her eyes.

"This kid will be a mess, won't it?" she said.

"I hope it looks like you," I said.

"Me too," she answered.

Her hug was all-encompassing.

"Your love for me is scary," I said.

"Love is easy," she said. "You just have to let it in."

Was I ready for it? Who knows? But it was right in front of me.

"We've got a long walk back," Amy said.

"We'll make it."

We kissed for a long time, but eventually, we started our journey back.

"You do realize I'm going to throw you in the water when your pregnancy is over," I said.

"I'm looking forward to it," she said.

Chapter Thirteen

– Looking for an escape route – August, 1995

"Having children is like having a bowling alley installed in your brain." — Martin Mull

I usually made it into work right at eight o'clock. On August 15th, the morning of our doctor's appointment, I was called into Paul Robeson's office at two minutes after eight.

Robeson was the chief editor at the magazine. He was my direct supervisor, and a tremendously fat, unbelievably lazy man.

"Brown, come on in, grab a cup of coffee."

"I don't want coffee," I said.

He looked at me as though my skipping coffee with him was an insult of some sort.

"Anyway, what's the biggest story in Connecticut sports these days?" he asked as he plopped his ass into his chair.

It was such an unbelievably easy question that I didn't think he was actually looking for an answer. Corey Magorey, the star basketball player at the University of Connecticut, had been arrested for breaking and entering and possession of a concealed weapon. At the arraignment, he broke down and told the world he had a cocaine habit that controlled his life.

"You do want to be a sports reporter, right?" Robeson asked.

"Yes," I said.

I shifted in the chair and looked to the floor.

"This is your chance to shine, my boy. We want you to chase down the story of addictions. Try talking with Magorey. Talk to the people at the drug hotline. Find out where an athlete in trouble goes for help. Tear the lid off the story and we'll run it on the cover."

A surge of adrenaline raced through my body. I was being handed the cover. It was a dying magazine, but it was the most important moment in my short career.

"I'll do my best," I said.

Robeson was all smiles. He stood to shake my hand and my eyes immediately went to a stain on the front of his white shirt.

"My Egg McMuffin got away from me this morning," he said.

Under normal circumstances I would have laughed, but with the doctor's appointment staring me in the face, and with the story already burning through my mind, this wasn't a normal day.

"You won't be disappointed," I said.

◊ ◊ ◊

Immediately, I understood that this wasn't just a spoiled athlete story. In what turned out to be the break of my life, I was able to get an interview with Magorey through one of Luke's countless connections. It turns out that Luke's brother had played high school ball with Magorey a few years earlier. I met Connecticut's 'Mr. Basketball' in the parking lot of a cafe on the edge of town.

Magorey was so gun-shy he wouldn't even enter the cafe. He bent his six-nine frame down to my window, and lightly tapped on the glass.

"Let's ride," he said. "I don't want to be seen."

I let him into my car. We were two completely different people. When he got through this legal battle, he would be back on the floor knocking down twenty-foot jump shots. He would go on to pro ball where he'd make millions of dollars, and I would go back to my boring life. Yet, that morning, we made a connection.

"You ever been addicted?" he asked.

I was driving around aimlessly. I had promised not to take notes or record the conversation. I was certain that I could get to the essence of the story without actually blasting Magorey as every other reporter had done.

"I've been addicted to a girl," I said.

Magorey laughed.

"Probably not the same thing," he said. "I been doing blow for ten years. Half my fucking life."

My heart sunk with a feeling of compassion.

"People tell me I'm throwing it all away, but I don't know what to do about it. My body aches for the shit."

I caught a side-glance at the man, and the idea of worshipping him as a basketball star was the furthest thing from my mind. He was telling me that he was virtually helpless.

"Did you try to get help?" I asked.

Again, he laughed.

"I'm not exactly anonymous," he said. "Since I started playing ball, I've been watched real close. Everyone loves me, but inside, I'm nothing but a failure. It kills me because I feel like I'm living my life outside my body."

I knew exactly what he was talking about.

"It's like you're doing what you're supposed to do but you don't feel it in your heart, right?" I said.

"That's right."

Magorey actually clapped his hands.

"And the thing is, I always seem to hide from it. When things get tough, I run to the drugs, man."

"I run to Claire," I said.

I hadn't meant to say it out loud, but it was there for consideration.

"We've got to face life head on," he said. "No one is going to hand us anything."

His admission opened the door. We talked about our hopes and dreams. We got to know each other as friends, and I told him about Amy and the baby, and my addiction to Claire. We spent a little over two hours in the car, and it might have gone on a lot longer if I didn't have the doctor's appointment. I drove back to the cafe, and the superstar athlete ducked out of my car and returned to my side window.

"I hope you got a story," he said. "Good luck today."

He poked his incredibly long fingers through the window and I shook his hand. It had been impossible for him to get help for his addictions. No one actually understood his mind, and down deep, no one actually cared. We both knew there were people who were reveling in his problems.

"If you want an ending," he said, "tell everyone that I'm going to face it. No more drugs for me, man; I'll beat it down."

I really wanted to believe him.

"Face your addiction, too," he said. He laughed loudly. "Maybe being addicted to a chick is the same thing."

I laughed with him. We shared a misery.

◊ ◊ ◊

I was running late, but I stopped at the apartment long enough to change clothes and check the answering machine. I was pulling a shirt over my head when I heard Claire's voice.

"Hey, stranger, what's going on? Don't you love me anymore?"

The sound of her voice dropped me into a sitting position on the bed. She was actually cooing, and my heart was firmly planted in my throat.

"You don't write or call to see if I'm lonely."

I heard Steven's voice in the background as he shouted out a hello.

"Steven says hello. He hasn't been feeling great, but then again, you wouldn't know that because you don't call. Anyway, get a hold of us. We got news. Love you. Bye."

I thought of Corey Magorey and his addiction to cocaine. I played the message three times. I missed her so badly that I was on the verge of tears. I wanted to tell her about the pregnancy and my big story. I wanted to feel her arm around my shoulder as she offered words of encouragement. I punched the number into the telephone, believing I'd tell her everything. Of course, when she answered, I chickened out.

"Hey," she yelled when she heard my voice. "Speak of the devil."

"What?" I asked.

"We were just discussing you."

"All good, I hope," I said.

The sound of her voice in my ear sent a shiver down my spine. I imagined myself as Corey Magorey with the cocaine exploding into my brain.

"We were talking about weddings," she said. "Steven bet me that you'd be next."

I swallowed hard. It was my chance to explain it all.

"Not unless you're available," I said.

She laughed. "I might be. Steven's had a stomachache for like three weeks now. I'm sick of him whining about it. I might shoot him."

"So, what's the news?" I asked.

"So much for small talk," Claire said.

I glanced at my watch. As much as I would have liked to chat, the reality was that I had to be at the doctor's in less than a half-an-hour.

"It's about a wedding," Claire said.

Claire hesitated as though I'd know what she was talking about.

"She said you wouldn't figure it out," Claire said.

"Who?"

"Your mother, goofball. She wanted me to call you. Your mother's something else. She still thinks we're ten years old and constantly together."

Oh, how I wished it were true.

"Why didn't she call me?" I asked.

"She was afraid, I guess. Are you all right?"

"Yeah, I suppose." I shook my head, and smiled. "It ain't every day that you hear your mother's getting married."

"Just remember, if you find someone to love in this world, you have to hold on tooth and nail. Be happy for your Mom, okay?"

We talked for a couple of minutes more, but I could only think of what she had said about holding on tooth and nail. Was there something I could have done to make it different for us?

◊ ◊ ◊

I met Amy in the parking lot. She skipped across the lot and met me in an embrace. She was wearing a tight black dress and an ear-to-ear smile.

"Are you ready, daddy?"

I kissed her gently and took her hand without a word. I was almost afraid of what might come out. This was a moment for someone else. I had no business leading this wonderful girl into the doctor's office.

A gorgeous, young, blonde woman led us into the waiting room. I immediately went to reach for an old copy of *Reader's Digest*, but at the last second, took Amy's hand instead.

"How was work?" she asked.

"I met Corey Magorey today," I said. "I've got a chance to gain the cover. He's a great story, but more than that, he's a good man."

"That's awesome," Amy said. She kissed me quickly. She was a little too excited for my taste, but that was understandable. She was excited about the child inside of her.

"I had the blood test. I've been so nervous all day."

We were silent for a moment as we considered how much our lives would change.

"Oh, yeah, my Mom's getting married. They're sending us plane tickets out to California."

Amy crinkled her nose and I saw concern in her eyes.

"I'm all right with it, but you have to go with me," I said.

Before I could finish the thought, the blonde called us front and center. We were ushered back into a waiting room where more stacks of old magazines awaited us.

"Why the hell do they do this?" I asked.

Amy shrugged in confusion.

"Every doctor's office in the world does it. You get comfortable in one waiting room and they come and get you and bring you down the hall to another one. It's not like we walked a mile to get to this room, why couldn't we have just stayed there?"

Amy still didn't know what the hell I was talking about, but she shut me up with a gigantic kiss. At that moment, Doctor Clark Gaines walked through the door.

"Isn't that how this started?" he asked.

We both laughed, but Gaines didn't wait around for us to say anything.

"The results are in, but I have a patient down the hall that I have to see for two minutes. I'll be right back."

He closed the door, and Amy's nervousness reached its peak.

"Have you figured out what we're going to do? We can't live with Luke anymore, and the baby will need a nursery. Do you want a boy or a girl? Do you want to find out? I want it all. I want a house with a white picket fence and two dogs."

The room was spinning out of control. The door being opened saved me from collapse.

"Do you still need to see the doctor?" the beautiful receptionist asked.

99

I shot a look at Amy, who shrugged.

"The test was negative, right? What else do you need?"

Amy actually screeched. It almost sounded like the noise Archie made when the car hit him all those years ago. To my credit, I pulled her into a hug before she actually broke down weeping.

"Go get the doctor," I said. "You didn't have to tell us like that."

The girl huffed as though I had slapped her and disappeared behind the door. Amy was crying hard, but the God's honest truth of it was that I didn't have a single thought on the matter.

◊ ◊ ◊

That night, Amy took a sleeping tablet and turned in early. I kept a small overhead lamp on in the kitchen and typed out the story of Corey Magorey. I wrote as I had never written before, and when I was done, I knew I had a masterpiece on my hands. The title of my article was inspired by the story of my life up to that point. As I wrote, I considered being the child of a divorced couple. I thought about Claire, Steven and Weird Henry. I put a face to the child that Amy wasn't carrying in her body. I imagined what it felt like to be loved like Corey Magorey, and how it felt to be vilified by the same people who cheered for you. I entitled the story, "*Addiction, despair, and a glimmer of hope.*"

Chapter Fourteen

– The Wedding – Part II –

"Marriage is like a bank account. You put it in, you take it out, you lose interest."
— *Professor Irwin Corey*

My mother's second wedding was a major event. To my growing astonishment, Keith was filthy rich and equally generous. They exchanged vows at Golden Gate Park, surrounded by flowers and a classical band. Mom was all decked out in white, which was pretty funny considering that her two sons were there.

Of course, I stood in the wedding along with Michael and Keith's two sons. Claire was my partner, and to be brutally honest, I wasn't quite ready for the sight of her. As wonderful as she looked in my mind, the real version was even better. She wore a light green dress with absolute radiance. Her bright eyes were so alive that I had to continually remind myself that we weren't husband and wife, and that I couldn't love her.

Given the fact that the wedding began shortly after our plane landed, I didn't see Claire until we made our short walk up the center aisle. The sun was shining, violins filled the air, and we hooked arms and began our journey.

"You look great," she whispered.

"There isn't a person at this reception looking at me right now," I said. "Did Amy come along?"

We were about halfway up the aisle. I wished it were a mile longer.

"Yeah, she's here."

"Can I steal you for a few minutes today?" Claire asked.

We reached the spot where we were supposed to break off.

"You never have to steal me," I said.

◊ ◊ ◊

Mom and Keith exchanged wedding vows written for the occasion. It was hard to hear, but my mother's vows consistently referred to the idea that they deserved to be happy in their love. Perhaps they did deserve happiness, but who ever got it?

I scanned the crowd looking for Amy. She was tucked deep in the back, side-by-side with Steven. My amazement upon seeing Claire was quickly overshadowed by astonishment as I took in Steven's appearance. His skin was pale and pasty, and from my vantage point at the head of the wedding, it was easy to see that he had lost at least twenty-five pounds. Still, Amy was leaning on his shoulder and whispering into his ear, so I understood that it was the same old Steven. Yet, what kind of stomachache did that to you?

The wedding concluded in just over an hour's time. The band waltzed us back down the aisle, and I met up with Claire again. She held tears in her eyes and before taking my arm she leaned in and kissed me on the cheek.

"You've made your mother the proudest woman in the world," she whispered.

I didn't know how to break it to her, but I hadn't done a damned thing. My mother's life with Keith was separate from mine.

"She deserves to be happy," I said.

Keith sprung for limos to take us to the Meridien Hotel in San Francisco for the reception. The ride took an hour, and with Steven and Amy joined at the hip, Claire was my companion. Sipping champagne in the back of a limo with Claire inches away was more or less my definition of heaven. We talked and laughed, and just when I was thinking that it might be the greatest day of my life, the roof caved in.

My relationship with Michael had changed through the years, and I couldn't put my finger on why. Perhaps it was because he had forgiven Dad and I truly hadn't. In any regard, we should have been closer. We stood side-by-side as the photographer snapped our pictures, but I really didn't know him any more.

"Have you seen Steven yet?" he whispered.

"Those ulcers are eating him up," I said.

"He's dying," Michael answered.

The photographer was asking me to smile, but Michael's words cut deep into my heart. It was just ulcers. Nobody actually died from a stomach problem.

"By the way, you should call Dad."

Michael was almost threatening me with his eyes. I turned and walked away.

Dinner was a choice of filet mignon or stuffed crab. I milled around a bit, but being in the wedding kind of strapped me to the front of the room. I mouthed a hello to Amy, but she was talking a mile-a-minute with Steven. It didn't matter; Claire was within arm's reach.

"Steven doesn't look so hot, huh?" Claire asked.

"What's the matter?" I asked.

She touched me lightly on the arm.

"He assures me that the doctor can control it. I don't know much about ulcers, but the medication should clear them up."

There was a glint of worry in her perfect eyes.

"We're trying to have a baby," she said.

I sipped my drink and smiled.

"Is Amy doing all right?" Claire asked.

Again, I smiled. She was asking me about major life issues and I was smiling at her like a semi-retarded child.

"It's got to be serious," she said. "You've been together for awhile."

"Why do they use the term 'serious'?" I asked. "Isn't that how they classify accident victims?"

Claire laughed heartily, but I knew she still wanted the question answered.

"It's more than serious, it's critical," I said.

I could have set it all out for consideration. I could have told her about the phantom pregnancy and the realization that my love for Amy was not a mere fantasy. Something made me hold my tongue.

"Hey," Amy called out.

She was hanging on Steven's frail-looking right arm.

"I've had seven gin and tonics," she said. "If you play your cards right, you'll get some tonight."

I avoided Claire's eyes and shook hands with Steven.

"I know. I'm skin and bones," he said. "Claire told you about the ulcers, huh?"

"How'd you get ulcers at twenty-four?" I asked.

"You should try living with her," he said.

Steven kissed Claire on the mouth. She eased into his hug, and I couldn't imagine life being anything but perfect with her.

"You got a minute?" Steven asked.

He led me to the patio bar where Michael waited with shots of Jack Daniels all in a row.

"A drink for old time's sake," Steven said.

"Did you tell him?" Michael asked.

We were alone at the bar, as it was nearing dinnertime and the other guests were searching for their seats.

"Tell me what? Hey, you shouldn't be drinking whiskey with stomach ulcers."

Steven's head went to the floor.

"They aren't ulcers," he said.

He raised his shot glass. "To Weird Henry."

I tapped glasses with Steven and Michael.

"If it isn't ulcers, what is it?" I asked.

"Drink first," Michael said.

I downed the shot and winced as I struggled to keep it inside.

"It's liver cancer," Steven said.

I started to retch and gag. My mind went completely blank and I struggled to keep my eyes off Steven's drawn face.

"But, Claire."

"Claire doesn't know," Steven whispered.

I was almost waiting for them to burst into laughter, but neither of them so much as smiled.

"I've been lying to her for a little over two weeks. I told Michael a while ago, but, I wasn't sure if you or Claire could handle it."

104

It didn't make sense. Claire was the one who solved the problems. How could he keep it from her?

The bartender filled our glasses. The waitresses were delivering the dinner salads.

"She's tough, but I don't want her to worry any longer than she has to," Steven said.

We slugged the shots down again. I was dizzy from the alcohol and on the verge of fainting from the sadness.

"It's not fair," I said.

"I'm not afraid of going," Steven said. "I just need to know you'll take care of her. I have to find that out before I tell her."

I pulled him into a hug. He was so thin that I thought he might just slide through my arms.

"How could she not figure it out?" I asked.

"She probably has some idea," Michael said, "but you believe what you have to believe to get through the day."

"I'm so sorry," I whispered to Steven.

"Just take care of Claire," he said.

He pressed his face into my shoulder. I tried to blink back the tears, but it was a losing battle. Everything had suddenly changed. Weird Henry was gone. Steven was dying, and Michael wouldn't know what to do with all of it.

The band took their positions to play the dinner music. The lead singer was going on about the day being perfect. He had no clue how wrong he was.

Chapter Fifteen

– It's got to be better than this –

"There's no such thing as inner peace. There is only nervousness and death." — *Fran Lebowitz*

Time doesn't wait for anyone. Life goes on around misery and pain. Three days after the wedding and Steven's horrible news, I was at my office awaiting my next assignment. Caroline, the over-worked and under-paid secretary paged me.

"Robeson wants you," she said.

My mind shifted to the Corey Magorey story. It was the only good thing going on in my life. I had sent the story to *Sports Illustrated*, and Robeson was no doubt calling me in to congratulate me.

Of course, he was eating when I walked in. He had a huge donut attached to his upper lip, and a telephone in his right ear. He waved to the chair in front of his desk.

I sat and searched the room for signs of anything other than reminders of his miserable life. He downed the donut and returned the telephone to its cradle.

"We're waiting on Tolliver," he said.

Tolliver was the owner of the pathetic magazine. I must have beamed because Robeson shook his head.

"It's probably not what you think," he said.

I had never actually met Richard Tolliver. The office gossip was that he was filthy rich and equally eccentric.

Tolliver rushed into the room and offered his hand. The thought that rushed to the foreground of my mind was that Tolliver could have passed for a member of the rodent family.

"It's nice to meet you," he said. "You did a fine job with the Magorey piece."

"Thanks," I said.

We sat and Tolliver quickly deferred to Robeson.

"The problem is, we got a call from *Sports Illustrated* today," Robeson said.

I shrugged.

"Are you trying to sell the story to them?" Tolliver asked. His eyes twitched when he talked, and again, I thought of a mouse.

I half-chuckled, and shrugged again.

"Well, yeah."

"You got two choices then. You can sell it to them or you can keep your job here," Robeson said.

I glanced at Tolliver. He held his palms up as if to ask me which it would be.

"First of all, that's one choice, isn't it?" I asked.

Robeson looked perplexed.

"I know that everyone always says you have two choices, and then lists just two options, but isn't a choice, by definition, a decision between two things?" I asked.

"What the hell are you talking about?" Robeson asked.

"Truthfully, it's not even one choice," I said. "I'll be going with *Sports Illustrated*. They have a few more readers than you."

"Then you're fired," Robeson said.

"And we might try to block the story," Tolliver added.

He wasn't going to block the story, and he knew it.

"Do what you have to do," I said.

Robeson eyed me as though I was making the worst decision in the world.

"By the way, Robeson, lay off the donuts. You're starting to look a little ridiculous," I said.

107

I was out of the office and out in the street in a matter of minutes. I had just added "unemployed" to my already impressive list of accomplishments.

◊ ◊ ◊

It would have worked out nicely had *Sports Illustrated* called me. I daydreamed of accepting an award as the world's greatest new sportswriter. Unfortunately, I also envisioned life on the streets, living from a shopping cart. My money supply was dwindling. Amy had offered to float me a loan, but I couldn't see clear to accept charity.

We were getting ready for the University of Connecticut basketball game in late November. Corey Magorey had opened the season with a string of twenty point games, and he was crediting me with his turnaround. Like me, he was waiting on the story to break, but unlike me, he was also waiting on criminal charges to be levied.

"So, we're sitting in the press box?" Amy asked.

She stood in front of the sink, applying her make-up. She wore only a long t-shirt, and from my vantage point on the couch, I caught a glimpse of the lower half of her body every time she moved in the right direction.

"Yeah, Magorey pulled a couple of strings."

"Doesn't that make you feel funny?" she asked.

She wasn't even looking at me, but I could tell she had something on her mind.

"Not really. In a couple of weeks, I'll be a celebrity around there."

Amy chuckled and shook her head.

"What?" I asked.

She started to say something and quickly stopped. I could almost see the wheels turning.

"Say what's on your mind," I said.

She stepped from the bathroom. She smiled, but I could tell that she wasn't jovial.

"It's been three weeks since Steven told you about the cancer, and you haven't so much as called him. It's been over two weeks since you lost your job, and you sit here every day watching soap operas."

So, it was all out in the open. She swiveled away and the shirt drifted with her, giving me a great shot of her naked bottom. I wasn't happy with what she said, but, of course, I looked.

"Steven said he'd call once he told Claire. *Sports Illustrated* is calling too, and I'm looking for work."

Again, Amy laughed.

"What?"

"My father used to joke with us," Amy said. "He'd tell us about living in a mansion, or taking a trip to Hawaii. He'd always end it by saying, 'We'll do all of those things and more when our ship comes in.'"

"That's funny," I said.

I turned away, realizing she was right. Like everything else in my life, I was dreaming of something that just might not come. I returned to the couch, thankful that our conversation was over. Yet, like any good woman, Amy came back for more. She pulled her jeans on and breathed deep to make the button.

"I'm not being critical, but our money is running low. We agreed to pool everything to make the rent."

"And I'm not carrying my share of the load," I said.

She sort of half-smiled again, and it embarrassed me more than anything else.

"I'll take the job at the sports bar," I said. "I can sling drinks for awhile."

She seemed pleased with the notion, and she wrapped her arms around my waist.

"Just do it until your ship comes in," she said.

I ducked out of her embrace.

"Come on, I'm just kidding."

Thankfully, the telephone rang. I picked it up and offered a gruff hello.

"Leo Brown, please," a young woman said.

"Speaking."

"Mister Brown, this is Carla Leone from *Sports Illustrated*. I've been asked to contact you regarding your feature story on Corey Magorey."

I could see the mast of the ship on the horizon.

"Yes?"

"Are you free to fly to New York on Tuesday morning to meet with the editors?"

I asked Carla to excuse me for a moment, and I cupped the phone.

"Um, Amy, dear, what's our schedule on Tuesday? *Sports Illustrated* wants to know if I'm free to swim out to meet a ship."

Amy shrieked and then screamed. Her unmitigated glee made my heart jump. I returned to Carla, who had no doubt heard the scream.

"Tuesday will be fine," I said.

"We'll express mail a ticket and expenses to you. Everything you need to know will be included."

I thanked her several times and met Amy in the center of the living room. We kissed for a long time, but, inexplicably, I thought of Claire.

◊ ◊ ◊

Magorey was all over the court. When the game ended, he totaled thirty-eight points and carried the team to victory. It was hard not to admire his game, but I stood more in awe of the way he was handling himself. He didn't pump his fist to embarrass his opponent. He didn't do any celebration dances, and his post-game interviews were full of praise for his coaches and his teammates. In a small way, I congratulated myself for making him see things a bit more clearly. I shook his hand outside the locker room, and introduced him to Amy.

"Wait for me to shower," he said, "we'll go to the sports bar and I'll get you that job."

"*Sports Illustrated* called," I said. "They're planning on running the story."

"That's great," he said. "I just hope they don't make me out to be a victim. I brought it all on myself."

"You'll be fine," I said. "Meet me after the game and we'll celebrate."

I was on top of the world when he smacked my hand, ignored the other reporters, and slipped back into the dressing room.

"You *are* going to make it," Amy said.

Just as I had thought of Claire when we were kissing, my mind turned to thoughts of Steven as I considered her words.

The 'Five-Star' sports bar was jammed pack with UConn fans. The thirty-five television sets were either replaying the game or broadcasting post-game interviews. I couldn't help but imagine my own face on the screen. If *Sports Illustrated* picked-up the article, I would be a top interview in town.

I fought my way through the crowd to the bar. Amy stayed close to the door, awaiting Magorey's arrival. I grabbed two beers and headed towards the door. It was unexplainable, but the celebrating students made my heart grow heavy. There was so much about life that was just unfair. Why was Steven suffering when his life was just supposed to be getting underway? What had he done to deserve any of it? Why did Weird Henry feel enough pain to end his life? Why couldn't I have a decent conversation with my father?

Without even seeing him, I knew he had arrived. The crowd sort of parted and Magorey stepped through. He caught my eye and offered a tremendous smile. Instantly, I knew he wasn't the same guy I'd met outside the locker room. He wrapped his huge arm around my shoulder and tried to lead me to the bar.

"Here's the guy who's going to make me a star," he said.

There were four other players with him.

"*Sports Illustrated* is printing the article about the misunderstood superstar," Corey said.

I felt sick. I smelled marijuana on his breath. Amy was beaming, and all eyes followed the huge superstar and the little, unemployed, sports reporter.

"I've got to go," I said.

"What's the matter?" Magorey asked. "Let's do some partying."

"It looks like you already did," I said.

They were announcing Magorey's arrival. The crowd broke into a round of thunderous applause.

"I got you the job," Magorey shouted. "Let's celebrate."

His eyes were already bloodshot, but I saw that he understood why I was upset.

"Awe, come on," he groaned.

I set my beer on the bar. I grabbed Amy's hand and turned my back on him. He laid a hand on my shoulder. I spun out of his grasp and headed for the door.

111

Clifford Fazzolari

In the parking lot, a crowd quickly gathered. Magorey was following close behind us, shouting for me to turn to him. I know that Amy figured I had gone completely off the deep end, but she didn't say a word.

"Man, what do you want from me?" Magorey said.

I spun to face him. He had cried out to me. He had played the part of a victim. I felt used and manipulated. Yet, his eyes begged me for acceptance. I grabbed his hand and led him to the back of the building. A few members of the crowd tried to follow, but Magorey's teammates kept them at bay.

"I smoked a half-a-joint," he said.

"You can't afford to do that," I answered. "The courts are considering what to do with you. Your team can suspend you. *Sports Illustrated* will can the whole deal if you get in trouble again."

"I was fired-up from the game. I had a good night, didn't I?"

"You don't get it, do you?" I shouted.

Magorey was like a child in front of the principal for the first time.

"All of this is bullshit. Those people don't love you. Your game isn't going to always carry you through," I said.

He bowed his head.

"It's about personal responsibility," I said. "If you don't give a shit enough to care for yourself, I can't help you."

It was impossible to imagine that he would accept such words from me, but he was nodding along.

"I'll squash that fucking article. I'll help them throw you in jail."

His eyes welled with tears.

"Why would you do that?" he asked.

"Because I'm worried about *you*. My best friend, growing up, is dying of liver cancer, and he doesn't deserve it. And you, you got the world by the balls, and you don't deserve that either."

I honestly would have walked away, but Magorey grabbed me from behind. For a brief instant, I thought he might throw me to the ground, but, instead, he pulled me into a hug.

"I've never had anyone really give a shit about me," he said.

Suddenly, I felt a little like Claire. She had always pulled me out of the whirlwinds of my mind.

"You have to stay on top of it," I said. "Those aren't your friends."

112

What an odd couple we made. The huge star cried onto my shoulder.
"I'll call you when I get back into town," I said.
"How's your addiction going?" he asked. He wiped the tears away.
I didn't answer.

◊ ◊ ◊

The story sold for a lot of money. I not only had the top feature story, I also had the cover. *Sports Illustrated* planned to evoke a lot of sympathy for Corey Magorey. I also left New York with a job interview as a sports columnist for the *New Haven Times*. As it turns out, the head editor had been schooled in New Haven.

Awaiting my flight from JFK, I telephoned Steven and Claire. Claire answered the telephone on the first ring.

"I sold the story," I said. "They're talking about giving me the cover."

"That's awesome," Claire said, but, I could tell that she had been crying.

"How are you?" I asked.

"Good. In fact, we're doing great. Steven wants to speak with you."

I heard her call his name, and Steven's voice came over the line a few moments later.

"It's time to tell her," Steven whispered. "Can you fly here?"

I immediately called Amy.

"I'll meet you there," she said.

"Actually, this is something I have to do on my own."

"Good luck," Amy said.

I could tell she was upset for some reason, but sooner or later we'd be able to smooth it out. I forgot to tell her about the sale of the story.

Chapter Sixteen

– Emotionally bankrupt –

"To get back on your feet, miss two car payments."— *Unknown*

Waiting for an airline to get their shit together is the most frustrating feeling in the world. I watched the departing flights screen as though it were a television set. Evidently, there was trouble with the weather in Buffalo. Whatever the cause, I was stuck at JFK for two hours longer than I expected. I used the time to take stock of what was happening.

Thinking about everything was scrambling my brain. *Sports Illustrated* was intent on waiting to see what happened when Magorey was sentenced. Steven evidently had a plan on how to break the news to Claire. I was almost completely out of money, and Amy was riding the wave, not sure where she fit in. Inexplicably, my mind kept shifting to thoughts of my father.

It had been quite awhile since we had spoke. It seemed he'd stopped trying to get me to validate his life with Margaret. While I had always been able to count on a telephone call every now and then, the calls had stopped. I wondered what he was doing with his life. Did he miss me at all?

The airport was crowded and in every anonymous face I saw evidence of the catastrophe of life. It all came down to how we reacted in a particular situation. Life was all about waiting for moments, and doing your best when your back was against the wall. I was flying home to confront a truly harrowing moment. The attendant called for final boarding to Buffalo and, I thought of the long trip back to Claire's side. It was an opportunity for me to establish the sort of man I would become. It was also a horrible shame.

◊ ◊ ◊

Steven met me at the gate. He had continued to deteriorate at an alarming pace. His skin was gray and seemed to be hanging on his bones. I pulled him into a hug, and I saw a large tear on his right cheek.

"Sorry about the delays," I said. "It drives me nuts to see the new time come up on the screen. I couldn't wait for the clock hands to move."

"Don't ever wish time away," Steven answered. "I used to be real impatient, but, lately, it's tough to waste time. That's the one thing I'm a little short on."

My heart sunk. In the end, we would all be fighting for a little more time. What else was there?

"I'll drive," I said.

"I got it," Steven answered. "I'm not in bad enough shape to let you do the driving. Remember Florida? I drove ninety percent of that trip."

"I offered to drive," I said.

"Remember when we crossed the border from Georgia to Florida?" he asked.

How could I forget it? We had pledged eternal friendship.

"This sucks," he said. "I always thought our kids would play together like we did."

It was up to me to react. I couldn't dwell on the illness. I couldn't talk of yesterday. His hope was fading away, but I had to keep his mind on the future.

"Can you imagine my kid in little league?" I asked.

Steven offered a side-glance and a slight smile.

"He'll be pissing his pants."

Our shared laughter was probably a little stronger then it would be under normal circumstances.

"She knows something's up," Steven said. "She's always known so much more about life. She was an amazing child, and she turned into an amazing woman."

"You don't have to convince me," I said.

115

"I got some drugs that control a lot of the symptoms," Steven said, "but she still sees it. I throw up a lot and all you really have to do is look at me to understand."

We were a few miles from their home. Claire and Steven had taken up residence just miles away from our childhood homes. They had never traveled far away from where it all began.

"So, why didn't you tell her?" I asked.

"Because it'll change everything," he said. "I wanted to hold onto the old Claire as long as I could."

◊ ◊ ◊

She was sitting in the center of the living room with Christmas cards spread out before her. She didn't look up when we came in, and evidently, Steven hadn't told her that I was coming home with him. She wore sweatpants and an old Buffalo Bills shirt. Her hair was wet, and her make-up had already been washed down the sink.

I cleared my throat, and her head came up quickly. We stood before her, wrapped arm-in-arm.

"Leo!"

She jumped into my arms, and I hugged her for all that I was worth. Through all of the years, she had protected me from the hurt, and I had made the trip knowing I was there to hurt her very badly. When our embrace was broken, the reality of it all came crashing down on her head.

"What's going on? I thought you were going back to Connecticut. What else did *Sports Illustrated* say?"

"I had the meeting. Everything's all set. I'm not sure when they'll run the story. They'll probably wait to see if he winds up in professional ball or a jail cell."

"You said he's a good guy," Claire said.

"He *is* a good guy, but sometimes you slip off the right track, you know?"

"As long as you catch yourself," Claire said.

Her voice trailed off and she looked from me to Steven and back to me.

"So, I guess you're here to help break the news," she said.

She nervously flicked at her long, blonde hair. Her eyes were already filled with tears.

"Well, let's do it right."

She sat on the edge of the couch and considered us for a moment.

"I've been thinking about how you'd tell me," she said.

Steven knelt in front of her. He stroked her hair, and kissed the side of her face.

I didn't know what to do. I felt as though I were intruding on a love that was too intense for me to ever understand. Tears were rolling down my cheeks, but I didn't seem to have the knowledge of how to brush them away.

"How much do you know?" Steven whispered.

"Everything," she said.

They cried in one another's arms for what seemed like an hour. I stood off by myself until they welcomed me into their embrace.

"We had planned on years of love," she whispered. "We just have to cram it all into the time we have left."

Chapter Seventeen

– And a baby makes two –

"If we see the light at the end of the tunnel, it's the light of an oncoming train." — Robert Lowell

I attended Corey Magorey's sentencing hearing. It was easily the most bittersweet moment of my life. Magorey was sentenced to five years probation. He would be able to continue his march towards pro basketball. I would have my *Sports Illustrated* story, and UConn still had their chance at the NCAA championship. Yet, he had committed a crime that would have earned a lesser man a prison sentence, and the reasons for the slap on the wrist were painfully evident.

The courtroom was packed solid. Corey's fans sat in the front row and almost dared the judge to harshly discipline their best chance at a national championship. I sat in the back row along with twenty or so reporters. Everyone was trying to get the scoop. I didn't let on that I had already stolen the lead story.

The judge's name was Adam Wells. Wells was a short, fat, pathetic-looking man. He sat on the edge of his chair as he addressed Magorey. In the most ridiculous of all scenarios, after passing sentence, he asked for Mr. Basketball's autograph.

Magorey shook my hand outside the courtroom. He asked me to contact *Sports Illustrated* to see what was happening with the story.

"I've really learned my lesson," he whispered.

I nodded and turned away. I wasn't sure I could believe him.

"By the way, Leo," Magorey shouted, "Happy birthday."

I had nearly forgotten my birthday. I turned and smiled.

"Want to go out and have a few?" he asked.

I looked at him as though he were absolutely crazy.

"I'm just kidding," he said. "Clean and sober from here on out."

I stepped into the chill of the December air. I remembered the day when I fought to prove the existence of Santa Claus. Maybe old Santa was still around. Magorey had been delivered a huge present. I said a quick prayer, hoping that Magorey was bright enough to recognize the gift and accept it with humility.

"I'm going to become a man," Corey announced to my back.

I couldn't help but think of my father. Once again, I considered calling him. Yet, my life was still in turmoil. Steven was in serious trouble. I still didn't have a job, and Amy was still waiting for a straight answer. I still didn't feel like a man.

◊ ◊ ◊

I entered the apartment a little before five o'clock. Amy's car wasn't in the drive and that meant I had to start dinner. Mindlessly, I moved to the refrigerator. I tossed the door open and a note drifted to the floor.

You aren't cooking, silly. I'm taking you out for your birthday.

I smiled at the note. She didn't let me down very often.

"Hey," she shouted.

My heart skipped a beat and I literally jumped. I spun around and the sight of her nearly dropped me to my knees. She wore a long, black gown. Her hair was neatly done up, and in her right hand were a dozen long stemmed roses.

"Happy birthday," she said.

I started moving to her, but she turned and ran from the room.

"Wait right there," she said. She set the roses on the kitchen table.

I picked up a single rose and held it to my nose. I wondered what the hell she was up to, but I couldn't stop grinning.

She was back in a flash with a huge cake. She set it beside the roses, and made for the door once more.

The cake was decorated like a basketball court. Scrawled at the bottom were the words, *Happy Birthday, Leo. You are my world.*

This time her approach was a bit more elegant. She stood in the doorway with a rose between her teeth and a bottle of champagne.

I didn't know what to say. I knew my mouth had dropped open, but my brain wasn't providing me with the words to encapsulate the moment.

"Nothing in the world prepared me for your heart," I whispered.

"Can I give you a birthday kiss?" she asked.

"Absolutely," I said.

Of course, it couldn't be that simple. She began a little dance around the apartment with the bottle of champagne.

"Not yet," she teased.

She uncorked the champagne and it ran down the side of the bottle. She laughed and put the bottle to her mouth.

I was moving towards her, but every time I got close, she backed away. She was at the door of the spare bedroom. She pushed the door open and stepped inside.

"You coming?" she asked.

I followed her inside, but what was waiting for me nearly dropped me to my knees. There was a desk in the center of the room with a brand new computer. Above the desk was a framed cover of *Sports Illustrated*. Corey Magorey was on the cover holding a basketball. Sweat dripped from every pore of his dark skin. *Addiction, despair, and a glimmer of hope*, was printed underneath.

"They over-nighted it to you. It won't hit the stands until Wednesday," she said.

I reached for it, but she stopped me.

"You got three copies," she said. "I only framed one."

She held the other two copies behind her back.

"I'll take that kiss first," she said.

I grabbed her around the waist and the magazines dropped from her hands to the floor. Magorey's photo was looking up at me, but I closed my eyes and kissed Amy. I tasted the champagne, smelled her perfume, and for the first time in a long time, thought of nothing other than the way she felt in my arms.

Amy sat on my lap and read me the article. Every other paragraph, we stopped long enough to sip champagne and kiss. Everything about the day felt like a dream. It was almost as though we were trapped within one of my fantasies. It would have been perfect had Claire...

I shook my head to get rid of the thought. Amy read on, oblivious to the sounds of my heart. When she reached the end of the article, she slipped her arms around my neck and offered the longest kiss of the night.

"I'm proud of you," she said.

"It's amazing that you love me," I answered.

Amy jumped from the chair as if she'd been fired from a cannon. It was all I could do to stop myself from dropping to the floor.

"We have to call Corey," she said.

She was halfway to the telephone when it rang.

"I know!" she screamed. "They sent us three copies too."

She held the receiver out to me.

"It's him. He's going crazy," Amy said.

Amy went looking for the champagne. I cleared my throat into the telephone.

"Leo! My main fucking man!" Corey cried out.

I heard the beep of our call waiting.

"It's awesome!" Corey shouted.

The line beeped again and I asked Corey to hang on a second.

"Fuck that other line. We're on the cover of *Sports-fucking-Illustrated*."

I clicked over, and Claire's voice filled the line.

"Hey there," she said. "Happy birthday."

"Thanks, um, listen, the story came out today. Magorey's on the other line," I said.

Claire didn't speak for a few seconds and with Magorey waiting, it seemed like a hundred years. Amy thrust the champagne bottle to me.

"Okay, but, you won't hear about *my* present," Claire said.

"No, what is it? I'll call him back."

"I'm pregnant," she said.

My heart sank and then rose all in a split-second.

"We've known for a while, but we wanted to tell you on your birthday."

My knees started to go weak. The call waiting beeped in and I imagined Magorey going crazy waiting for me to pick up. Claire's voice crackled with emotion as she told me her story. Amy's arms were around my waist. The

Clifford Fazzolari

taste of champagne was on my lips, and I kept looking at the cover of the magazine.

"Happy birthday, Leo," Steven said.

His voice was weak, and all at once, my feeling of euphoria vanished. His wife was having a baby that he would likely never see.

"I did it man. I'm going to be a father," he said.

"Congratulations," I said. "It's the best news I ever heard."

Tears stung the back of my eyes. Amy's arms were wrapped around my waist, and all I could think was that life was unbelievably ridiculous.

I didn't have a lot of time for my pity party.

"I'm going to beat this," Steven said.

"I have no doubts," I answered.

Amy massaged the lower half of my body. I struggled to break free although I wasn't sure that's what I wanted.

"They gave me some new drugs," Steven said. "I actually look forward to waking up in the morning."

"That's awesome," I said.

"And there are experimental things they can do now. I'm going to make it. I'm going to hold my baby."

"You'll watch him get his high school diploma," I said.

We let the conversation end naturally.

"Claire wants to talk to you again," Steven said. "I'll see you soon, buddy."

In the moment while they transferred the telephone, I thought of their love and how they deserved more.

"We'll get through this," Claire said. "He's going to beat this. What are we without hope in our hearts? Love's a powerful drug. It'll be a great healer."

For a moment, I almost believed her.

◊ ◊ ◊

Corey stopped by about an hour later with a case of beer, eight huge lobster tails, and the team point guard, Robbie Dillon. He held the beer up for inspection.

"Do you think I can have one?" he asked.

122

His big, dark eyes were almost pleading with me. For some reason, he wouldn't open the beer until I gave him the okay.

"I'm not your mother," I said.

"This is a special occasion," he said. "There isn't another man on the cover of *SI* this week."

"Yeah, but, you have to remember why you're on there," I said.

Amy was on my lap, kissing the side of my neck. The champagne was making me a bit light-headed. His puppy dog eyes begged me for the beer.

"It's not beer that bothers me," he said. "Come on, man, it's your birthday."

"Are you going to beat this thing?" I asked.

"Yes," he said.

"Are you going to be an all-star?"

"You know it."

He slapped my hand and let out a yelp. I dangled the beer out to him. Perhaps he had turned a corner in his life. He swiped the beer from my hand.

"Are you going to bring lobster tails when you're making a zillion dollars a year?"

He laughed and slapped me hard enough on the back that Amy nearly fell from my lap. I took a healthy swig of beer and tried to get it straight in my mind. Chances were that we were all trying to fool ourselves. Amy was dreaming that we'd be together forever. Magorey and Dillion were dreaming of pro basketball. Steven and Claire were dreaming of a future together with their new child.

Me? I wasn't dreaming. Somehow, I knew that it could all turn sour. Magorey raised his glass.

"Addiction, despair, and a glimmer of hope," he saluted.

We clanked glasses and downed the alcohol.

Maybe, that's what all of this meant.

Chapter Eighteen

– My fear of the end –

"While you're saving your face, you're losing your ass."
— *Lyndon Johnson*

I sat center stage on press row all through the 1992-93 NCAA basketball season. During that campaign, Corey Magorey turned the college sports world on its ear. Magorey was clean and sober and playing ball as though he were the second coming of Magic Johnson. He averaged thirty points a game, and the University of Connecticut was undefeated. I was caught in a dream season as I endured a personal nightmare.

On February seventh, Magorey scored forty-three points as Connecticut won their twenty-sixth game of the season. I hustled back to the newsroom with my notes scribbled on a yellow pad. I crashed through the front door and nearly collided with Amy.

"What're you doing here? I've got a deadline," I said.

"It's not good," she answered.

Life was about to rear its ugly head once more. The worry in her eyes scared the living shit out of me.

"Claire called. Steven had an allergic reaction to the new medicine. She's a wreck. You have to go."

The lobby seemed to be spinning. I wasn't sure if I should head to my office or run back out through the doors. My editor was probably already screaming for my copy.

"What the hell should I do?"

I held the notes out as proof that I was positively screwed.

"Write the story," Amy said, "I'll get your plane tickets arranged."

"Are you coming?" I asked.

For the first time, I read actual sadness in her eyes.

"I can't," she said. "I can't watch you comfort her. I know how you feel, but I just can't watch it."

It wasn't the time for this discussion. I shrugged as though she were being totally ridiculous.

"All right then," I said.

I should have hugged or kissed her. Instead, I ran for the elevators.

"I'll look for the earliest flight out of Hartford," she said.

Again, I should have thanked her.

The words to the story came rushing out of me. I had been glorifying Corey Magorey for so long that it came naturally. For a little over an hour, I blocked out thoughts of Steven. I wasn't sure if he'd be dead when I got to Buffalo. I chronicled the story of the game as though I had a Corey Magorey highlight reel playing in my head.

I handed in the first draft.

"Is it perfect, cover boy?" my editor, Jack Russell, asked.

"Fix it if it isn't," I answered. "My best friend from back home might be dying."

It pained me to say the words. I fought back the tears, and Russell put a hand on my shoulder.

"I'm sorry," he said. "You do what you have to do."

The son-of-a-bitch was already reading over the copy. He couldn't have cared less if everyone I ever knew had died.

"I'm out of here," I said.

On the way to the airport, I used my cellular phone to get ahold of Claire. She was absolutely frantic, and it shook me to the core.

"He took his medicine and went to bed," she choked out. "Immediately I knew he wasn't breathing right. I couldn't wake him up."

She was sobbing uncontrollably.

"He's in a coma. They can't even tell me if he's going to live or die."

"It'll be all right," I said. "I'll be there as soon as I can."

"Hurry up," she said.

I drove to the Hartford airport as fast as traffic would allow. The lights of the passing cars hypnotized me into a trance. My mind flashed picture after picture of a grieving Claire.

The telephone rang and I hit the hands-free button. Amy's voice filled the car.

"You're leaving at 12:35 from gate 100. Don't miss it, either; the next flight isn't until seven."

The dashboard clock read seven minutes after twelve and I was a good thirty miles away.

"Shit! That might not be good enough. I can't drive a hundred miles an hour!"

Amy was silent.

"You there?" I asked.

"Yeah, I'm here," she said. "It's the best I could do."

I stomped hard on the accelerator and two cars moved out of my way.

"Just be careful," Amy said.

"He *has* to be all right," I said.

"Do you know when you'll be back?" Amy asked.

I was disgusted with all of it.

"I have no idea. I imagine if he dies, I'll have to stay a little longer."

"Don't even say that," Amy said.

Her voice cracked just enough to tell me that she was crying. Unfortunately, I didn't have time to worry about how she was feeling.

"I was just trying to plan my schedule," she said.

And that's when I said it.

"I don't give a shit about you right now."

The line went dead. The plane was scheduled to leave in twenty-three minutes, and I was covering ground.

The taxi dropped me at the front doors of Buffalo General Hospital. I didn't have time to stop at the front desk. I took the escalator steps two at a time and navigated the arrows leading me to where they brought in the next batch of people to die. I used the wall telephone in the waiting room to inquire about Steven's status, but the bitch on the other end of the line wouldn't tell me anything. I was halfway through my little temper tantrum when an elderly lady cleared her throat to bring me back to the real world.

"There was a pretty, young girl waiting for him," she said.

"Yeah, that's Claire. Where is she?" I asked.

The woman paused as though I had asked her for the meaning of life.

"Do you know where she is?" I asked.

The woman cleared her throat again, and then leaned and spit into a handkerchief.

"I know," she said, "but I'm not sure if I want to tell you."

I sighed heavily. I was as frantic as I'd ever been in my life and this lady wanted me to work for it.

"I've been talking to her for three hours," the woman said. "It took me a long time to calm her down. I'm not sure if I want you getting her all worked up again."

It was almost laughable. I was there to comfort Claire.

"I've known her all my life," I said. "I'm her best friend."

The old broad assessed me with her dying eyes.

"You're Leo, right?"

My legs were wobbly.

"Sit a moment," she said.

I sort of flopped into the seat next to her.

"I'm Ethel Campbell."

I thought about shaking her hand, but imagined coming into contact with her soiled handkerchief.

"I know all about you," she said. "Leo, remember, life's a long road."

I wasn't sure I was up to the conversation, but I felt powerless to resist.

"You'll do a lot of smart things and just as many dumb things along the way."

It seemed that she was talking to herself.

"I've lived eighty-seven years," she said. "I know love when I see it."

I cupped my hands and stared at the floor.

"That Claire is one special lady."

"I know," I whispered.

"She loves Steven with her whole heart."

I knew that too. Yet, I loved Claire just as much.

"He's in a coma. But he'll make it. For some reason, I know that."

I nodded. Ethel slid a bony hand on top of mine.

"But Claire's going to have to face it up to it. She's going to have to make peace with this."

I felt tears sting my eyes. I wanted to brush them away, but her grip was powerful on my hands.

"She's going to need your love too, but she's afraid to ask for it. If you love her as much as you think you do, you'll have to make that love real for her."

I shook my head as though the woman had suddenly gone senile.

"She's afraid of interfering with Amy. She doesn't want to get in your way."

"That's ridiculous," I whispered. "It's Claire. I'd do anything for her."

Ethel pulled her hands away. She spit into the handkerchief once more. For the first time, I saw that she was in a wheelchair. Her legs were covered with what looked like a homemade blanket.

"My husband of fifty-two years is behind those emergency room doors," she said. "Anthony's been on life-support for three days now. If they pull the plug, he'll expire."

My heart was breaking. I had rushed through the night to be by Claire's side, but it felt right to wait it out. I breathed much easier, but the tears continued to fall.

"Isn't that a weird term?"

"What's that, Ethel?" I asked.

"Expire," she said. "It makes him sound like a library card, or a magazine subscription."

I heard the ticking of the wall clock. Time just kept moving on.

"I know I should be happy with the time we've shared, but I want a few more days," Ethel said. Her cries were soft and controlled.

"Anthony didn't want to be kept alive by a machine, but I don't have the guts to do it yet. Maybe tomorrow."

She dabbed her eyes with the handkerchief. I saw her less as an old lady and more as the loving person that she'd been all of her life.

"I said the same thing yesterday," she said.

She was trying to tell me something, but was allowing me enough time to figure it out for myself.

"It's hard to let love go," she said, "but sometimes, it's exactly what we have to do."

It hit me like a ton of bricks. Steven was in a coma, and Claire was worried about my lifelong obsession with loving her. She needed me by her side, but she wanted to guard my feelings.

"What should I do?" I whispered.

"Continue loving them," Ethel said. She pressed her eyes shut and a tear rolled down her wrinkled cheek. "It's the craziest thing I've ever seen. That woman is going to lose her husband way before she's supposed to, and she's worried about how it'll affect you."

I gazed at the floor as though the answer to all of it was written on the tiles somewhere.

"She's waiting for you in the cafeteria."

It took an incredible effort to lift myself out of the chair.

"One more piece of advice," Ethel said.

I leaned in to hear her. Deep down, I understood that I was getting a life's lesson that I wouldn't forget.

"What is it?" I asked.

"Don't shut Amy out. She doesn't deserve that."

I knew right then and there that Ethel's words came straight from Claire.

◊ ◊ ◊

Except for Claire, who sat at the table in a corner of the room, the cafeteria was empty. She met me in the center of the room and we held our embrace for a good three minutes.

"Thanks for coming," she said.

I waved the thought away. Ethel's words were still ringing in my ears, and I prayed to God for the ability to make it seem natural.

"Do you want another coffee?" I asked.

She nodded.

I slid a dollar bill into the vending machine and it spit it back out at me. I repeated the sequence five times until I felt like kicking in the front panel on the machine. I felt Claire's eyes on me the whole time, and I imagined her wondering how I had become such a loser. It really might have been funny in another place and time.

"We put a man on the freaking moon and we can't make a machine that recognizes a perfectly good dollar bill."

I said it loud enough for Claire to hear, and the sound of her laugh made me warm inside.

Thankfully, on the seventh try, the machine accepted my money.

"It was an allergic reaction to the medication," Claire said. "Doctor Bogner said that the next twenty-four hours are crucial."

"How's he been?" I asked.

The question sounded funny to me. It was almost as if I were a reporter on the scene at the Lincoln assassination who might have asked Mrs. Lincoln what she thought of the play. Claire glossed right over it.

"Good," she said. "Actually, great, in fact. We've spent a lot of time talking about the baby, you know. Yet, it's hard to look forward."

"You know, Weird Henry once told me that he couldn't plan for the future because he knew he was going to die. In the end, I think that's what killed him."

Claire seemed a bit confused. Weird Henry had died at his own hand. It was hardly the same thing.

"You guys have a future," I said. "Steven knows that. He'll come out of this."

As Claire cried, she looked away from me as though she were ashamed for some reason.

"How are you?" I asked. "You need to stay strong."

She nodded and smiled. Even in grief, her beauty was overwhelming.

"God has a plan for me. He's not giving me more than what I'm supposed to handle."

◊ ◊ ◊

Those were sixteen of the longest hours I ever spent. Steven was shut-off from the rest of the world, but I spent a lot of time at his bedside, trying to coax him back to life. He was skinny and nearly unrecognizable, but he looked so peaceful. Claire had taken up residence on the other side of the bed, and although we talked about our lives, we never escaped what was happening in front of us.

In the middle of it all, I telephoned my father. I wanted to tell him that I was becoming a man. He needed to know that I was facing my fears and living my life the right way. Margaret answered, and it took him a good five minutes to get to the telephone.

"Hi, Leo," he said.

"Dad, I'm in Buffalo."

"That's great," he said.

It dawned on me that he didn't sound so good. It was almost as though he were talking to me from underwater.

"Steven's pretty sick," I said.

"So am I," he answered.

He coughed lightly and my mind struggled with this new information.

"What's wrong?" I asked.

"Nothing. Bad cold, I guess."

He coughed once more, and I was mildly agitated by the fact that he could compare his cold with Steven's coma.

"Why don't you stop and see us," he said.

"I will," I promised.

"I have to go to the doctor's in a few minutes, but we'll be home later tonight."

I could feel the receiver pressed tightly against my ear. I don't know why, maybe it was the stress of the past few days, but I felt like crying.

"I'll swing by," I said.

"Good, we can have a beer and finish that conversation we started," he said.

He coughed again, and hung up without so much as a good riddance.

At four in the afternoon, Steven stirred back to life. He cleared his throat and let out a small groan that was music to our ears. Claire bent over the bed and kissed him on the mouth. She was crying but Steven was somehow oblivious to the fear that he had caused.

"Why am I so tired?" he asked.

"You shouldn't be. You've been sleeping for awhile." I said.

He turned to look at me. A smile creased his lips, and it made the entire trip worthwhile.

"My man, Leo," he said. "I knew you'd never let me down."

I offered him water and he happily accepted. Claire went out to get Doctor Bogner. She actually skipped from the room. I realized that the highs and lows of Steven's illness might actually kill her.

"I thought you were a goner," I said.

"I'm not going out easy," he answered.

It was exactly what I needed to hear.

Later on, it became painfully evident that I needed sleep and a shower. I had dinner with Claire in the hospital cafeteria, but I knew I was nearing the end of my stay. We were alone in the waiting room. Steven was sleeping comfortably.

"My parents are coming in a little while," she said. "I don't know if Steven's mother is coming down, but I don't have the strength to worry about it."

Suddenly, it hit me.

"What happened to Ethel?" I asked.

Claire bowed her head.

"No," I said.

"They pulled the plug right after Steven woke up."

Claire tired to speak again, but the deep sobbing stopped her. I pulled her into a hug. It took her a moment, but she finished the story.

"Anthony died in five minutes. She's been sitting in the room with him since. Her family has been trying to get her out of there, but she doesn't want to leave."

"Life sucks," I said.

Claire shook me off. She wiped away a tear, and reached for my hand.

"No one said it'd be easy," she said, "but life doesn't suck, Leo. Life's a gift. You have to appreciate it."

I could hardly believe my ears.

"How can you be so strong?" I asked.

"I'm not," she said, "Ethel told me that."

◊ ◊ ◊

I honestly didn't have a place to go. I contacted the airport and arranged for an afternoon flight out. In the meantime I needed sleep. I took a cab to the airport and rented a car. I drove to my father's house, but for one reason or another, I couldn't make myself walk up the drive.

I parked the car across the street and stared at their front window for over an hour. I imagined the life they had made together. My father's face as it had been when I was a child appeared in my mind. I realized that, aside from our telephone conversation, it had been over a year since even a single word had passed between us. In some ways, I really did miss him. Yet, I didn't have the energy tonight.

"Life's too short to hold grudges," I whispered to the interior of the car. I was too tired.

◊ ◊ ◊

At a little after four o'clock in the morning, my cellular telephone rang. I scrambled in the dark trying to find it. Amy's voice filled my ear.

"I'm coming in," she said.

"You don't have to," I said. "Steven's doing all right. They're talking about sending him home in a few days."

"Leo, I guess I'll come right out and say it. Your mother just called. Your Dad had a heart attack."

I bolted upright in bed. Why hadn't I gone into the house?

"When? How? Where is he?"

"Leo, he didn't make it. I'll be there in a few hours."

I remembered it all as if it had happened yesterday instead of years ago.

He shook his head again as though I were the dumbest man on the face of the planet.

"Some day you'll know what it's like to have a relationship," he said. "At least I hope you will."

I shrugged, and slammed down half my second beer in one large gulp.

"I'd rather not have one than screw one up," I said.

He slammed his fist down on the table. The twelve-pack actually bounced in place.

"I hope you become a man someday," he said. He was in a full-fledged rage, and I honestly couldn't blame him.

133

"*Don't worry about it. I'll become a man,*" I said.

"*Yeah, maybe,*" he said, "*but I'll probably be dead before that happens.*"

Chapter Nineteen

- Losing my religion -

"The trouble with born-again Christians is that they are an even bigger pain the second time."
— *Herb Caen*

The truth of the matter was that I had always seen my father through the eyes of a six-year-old. I never actually considered that he might not be around for me to blame. Yet I didn't burst into tears. Neither did I grab the telephone and offer my sympathies to Margaret.

Instead, I sort of fell from the bed and stumbled towards the shower. It took me a couple of minutes to decipher the hot and cold water controls. In fact, I spent the entire shower trying to find a comfortable balance as I tried to figure out how I would ever make myself clean.

I wanted to picture him playing catch with me in the backyard. I wanted to see his eyes as he offered worldly advice about how to live the right way. I wanted to remember a sign of affection. I just couldn't recall a time when he'd told me he loved me.

Stepping from the shower, I caught my naked reflection in a steamed mirror. I could have called him, too. We might have been able to talk it out. Perhaps we could have salvaged something.

I threw a punch at my reflection, and sobs of regret shook me from head to toe.

"You're wrong, Claire. Life does suck."

Twenty minutes later, I pulled into the spot across the street from my father's house. There was a single light on in the kitchen and a couple of times, I caught Margaret's form as she passed the front window. How could I honestly be expected to comfort her? In a matter of hours, her support would be there. I imagined that friends would soon surround her. Michael was on his way into town, as were Amy and Mom. All of the people who had loved Dad would step to the plate and offer their everlasting help and support. I just had to go first.

The walk up the driveway was the longest of my life. When I got within ten steps of the door, an overhead light went on, and I heard a small dog barking inside. Margaret opened the door a crack, and I stepped inside without a word.

I hugged her to my chest. She was softly crying, and her embrace was strong.

"He hadn't felt well for a long while," she said.

"I didn't know," I said.

The dog sniffed my leg and did a circle dance around me. I brushed him away.

"He'd been acting strange, but I just let it go."

I guided her to a chair at the kitchen table. Margaret was no longer the woman who had stolen Dad away. Her face was drawn. There was gray in her hair, and her body had rounded. We were virtual strangers, but we needed one another. The dog found a spot on the floor beside her chair. Suddenly, I was happy that she had the mutt's companionship.

"We went to the doctor today. They said everything was all right."

She was wiping tears from her eyes. It was a long while before she spoke again.

"I drove him to the hospital tonight. They said they'd check him out. A couple of hours later, I was dozing in the lobby, and they called me to the emergency room. They said he died in his sleep. I stayed there for another few hours, but there was nothing I could I do. I just came back here alone."

She recited it as though it were a speech that she'd practiced a hundred times, and she probably had.

"I thought he was a better fighter than that," she said.

They were words that I hadn't expected.

"He just gave up for some reason," she said.

136

I pictured him at the kitchen table, with the glasses on the edge of his nose, laughing at me as I discovered the truth about Santa Claus. I imagined him as my little league baseball coach. I remembered when he slapped the two hundred dollars on the table so I could go to Florida for spring break.

"He would've fought it," I said.

Margaret bowed her head.

"I loved him a lot, you know," she said.

"I know."

"He loved you too."

I guess I'd always known that. Yet, for one reason or another, I hadn't accepted his new life.

"Your father was a good man," Margaret said. "I wish you would have realized that."

Suddenly, I needed a drink. I knew that he had probably died with beer in the refrigerator, and I couldn't imagine him being happy about that. I sort of half-smiled as I considered it. Sure enough, there were seven or eight beers stacked in the back corner. I twisted the cap and slugged down a quarter of the beer.

"Don't get me wrong," Margaret said. "He wasn't a saint."

If she had noticed the beer, she wasn't letting on.

"He was so stubborn."

"Me too," I said.

I hoisted the beer to the ceiling in salute.

"He wasn't happy about the way things were with you, but he wanted the best for you," Margaret said. She didn't even try to hold back her tears.

I slugged down the rest of the beer and returned to the refrigerator for another. I don't think I had ever finished a beer so quickly.

"He left you a letter," she said. "He wrote it a few months ago. I was supposed to deliver it to you if anything ever happened."

Her slippers shuffled against the kitchen floor. She went to a drawer in the bureau and returned with two white envelopes. She slid mine across the table. Michael's name was emblazoned across the one she kept in front of her.

"How old was he?" I asked. "I mean I should know, but I don't."

"He turned fifty three months ago. He waited for you to call."

I took the beer and two others, kissed Margaret on the right cheek, and headed for the door.

"I'll be back in a little while. Try to get some rest. I want to read this alone."

"I understand," Margaret said.

It was hard getting out the front door. This wasn't the way it was supposed to end. We should have made amends all those years ago. Outside, I clutched the envelope to my chest and looked to the sky. Tears filled my eyes. There wasn't a star to be found.

◊ ◊ ◊

I sat in the car and watched as the sun peeked over the horizon. I was parked across from the house where I'd grown up. It was a house that my mother and father had purchased together. Their hearts were set on a world different from the one that they produced. From where I was sitting, I could see clear down the road that I had traveled as I grew up.

"Son-of-a-bitch, Dad," I said.

I twirled the envelope around and around. The most pitiful part of the entire morning was that the beer tasted good. I was about ready to bag everything that the day had to bring for the chance to get shit-faced.

It wasn't that he was dead and I felt guilty about how our relationship had played out. It was more about the fact that he was gone. Where the hell had he gone? Would he come back as a salamander? Would he just rot in the ground? Would he be playing a harp on a freaking cloud somewhere, or turning logs over in the fires of hell?

It was just another pack of lies. It was another freaking Santa Claus story in the most precious situation of all. Where would Steven be going? Why did Dad get out with a simple heart attack while Steven would have to suffer for months? Why did Steven get advanced notice of his closing while Dad's curtain was drawn all in one swift motion? Who the hell knew? Maybe I wouldn't make it through the day, or the week.

Reluctantly, I tore at the envelope. I was down to a beer-and-a-half and I didn't want to read the letter without a beer to chase it.

Leo - you're reading this because I have died, and we never had a chance to make amends. I'm sorry for that. This is a real cowardly way or

138

doing things, but I wasn't sure how to handle it. I never really knew what to say to you because you always stopped me dead in my tracks. Don't worry about it. I may have done the same thing in your shoes. The thing is, I never meant to abandon you. I always believed we could do everything that a normal father and son do, but we live in some tough times. I didn't marry your mother with the intention of divorcing her. I had expectations, as did she, but when it all came apart, we wanted different things. I remember the day you were born, and how proud it made me to be a father again. I prayed I would be the kind of man you could look up to, and in that respect, maybe I've failed you. I hope you can find it in your heart to see clear to how I truly felt about you. I loved you as much as I loved myself. I just didn't know how to show you.

Leo - In the past year or so, I've come to grips with my life. I've been able to categorize where I have succeeded and where I have failed. Along with Michael, you are my greatest contribution to the world. I'm sorry for having failed you in any way. As you make your way through this world, just remember to love with all of your heart. Your success depends only on what you feel inside. I've always meant to tell you that you've grown into a fine, young man.

Dad

◊ ◊ ◊

I read the note three times as I drained the last beer. Tears streamed down my face, but I felt more of a cleansing than a sorrow. I rested my head on the steering wheel. The sun was shining brightly and it glistened off what was left of the snow. I closed my eyes and, unbelievably, began to drift towards sleep. All at once, the passenger side door opened and closed. Without even opening my eyes, I knew who had slid into the seat beside me. I felt Claire's hand on my shoulder.

"We'll get through this," she whispered.

Her lips brushed against the side of my face, and I turned and pulled her into a full embrace. I cried like a three-year-old.

"First Weird Henry, then Steven, and now Dad. What's going on?" I cried.

"We're living," Claire said. "Life gets in the way sometimes."

◊ ◊ ◊

I'm not sure exactly who had the idea, but I knocked on the rectory door and waited for Father Peter Vickery to answer. It was the morning of the funeral, and while everyone was gathered at Margaret's, I was trying to understand the great beyond.

Father Peter didn't look much like a priest. He was probably no more than thirty-five-years-old, and he was as handsome as a movie star. It was a poorly kept secret that he played a lot of golf and drank a few beers on occasion. Yet, there was also no denying the passion of his commitment. Margaret had explained that his masses were so well attended that they had to provide extra seating, even on regular Sundays.

"So, you're David's boy? I'm sorry about your Dad. He was a good man."

I wasn't sure if I should admit that he probably knew him better than I. He shook my hand, and guided me down a narrow hallway into the rectory.

"So, you have a few questions, right?"

I wasn't sure he was looking for me to answer, as we had already discussed as much. He directed me into his study, and it wasn't anything like I had imagined. Sure, there was a crucifix hanging over the desk, but there were also professional photographs of every sports hero in the world. He had also framed the cover of *Sports Illustrated* with Corey Magorey on the cover. He pointed to it.

"Before we get started, you have to tell me what he's like. Is his life as full of turmoil as the article makes you believe?"

"Yes, and it was the perfect story for me to write," I said. "I felt his hope, his addiction, and his despair."

"He's a terrific ballplayer."

Father Peter was absolutely beaming.

"Yes, and that's what gets me about all of this. People bow to Magorey because he can put a ball in a hoop, but he's done some lousy things. My father's in a pine box and he left me a note saying that success came from inside."

140

Father Peter settled into the seat behind his desk. He held a smirk on his face that made me a bit uncomfortable, so I scanned above his head at the shots of Larry Bird, Joe DiMaggio, and Rocky Marciano.

"So what do you think life is all about?" he asked.

"That's why I'm here," I said. "I don't have a freaking clue."

Father Peter offered a hearty laugh that shook a couple of pictures behind him.

"I've got a void in my heart that I can't seem to fill. I'm always looking for something that isn't there. I'm always daydreaming about how I could make things better, and I don't know if I'll ever be happy. Now, you add death to the mixture, and I'm absolutely clueless."

Father Peter took down the photograph of Corey Magorey. He studied the man's face for a long time.

"There's a sadness in his eyes," he said. "Do you see it?"

Silently, I wondered if maybe Magorey had been high for the photograph. Perhaps it wasn't sadness, but marijuana.

"You kind of have that look, too."

"I'm just questioning things," I said.

"And there's nothing wrong with that," Father Peter said. "I'm not going to give you a huge speech about religion and how the Catholic Church can save you. You know all of that. I'm not going to quote the Bible to you and explain how you can be saved from yourself."

"Good. That's nauseating," I said.

Father Peter laughed once more.

"What I am going to tell you is that you'll find your way, just as I suspect Corey Magorey will."

"What makes you say that?"

I returned to the chair in front of the desk. My eyes skipped to a ball signed by each member of the 1977 New York Yankees.

"My faith tells me that God has a plan for you. You've talked about imagining how things should be, but if you look hard enough, you'll find yourself a real life. It might be right in front of you. It might be another thirty years down the road, but life isn't anything but a journey. You have free will to choose between right and wrong. There's a saint and a sinner residing in your heart, and you can be either one at any given moment."

141

It was my turn to smirk. He sounded so much like Claire that I nearly burst into laughter.

"What I'm saying is, keep going as you're going. Love and lose, love and win, dust yourself off and love again. We used to say that at the seminary."

He waved his hand at me.

"Anyway, I can tell you that your father's soul has been saved. I can promise you that there's eternal life, and that God loves us. I'm certain that we'll be judged at the right hand of the Lord."

He was starting to slip into something of a preacher's chant.

"I can offer you eternal redemption and a chance to save your soul. I hold the key to your happiness and I can open the window to your heart. And I know that you'll be saved. Do you know how I know that?"

I shrugged.

"Do you know how I know that Jesus loves you and will make your life worth living?"

He was waiting for some sort of response. "How?" I whispered.

He folded his hands in front of him, and sweetly smiled. Slowly, he brought his hand up, and pointed his index finger to his chest.

"Because it's right here," he said. "Everything I believe is in my heart. My real life starts and ends with what I know is right."

He allowed the thought to sink in. I glanced at a photograph of Michael Jordan.

"I'm just a normal guy," he said. "I always thought Jordan was overrated."

"Me too," I whispered.

"But that's what makes life fun. Your father died too young. Steven's illness is just plain tragic, and who knows? Maybe you'll spend the rest of your days trying to figure out what's in your heart. The thing is, deep down, you already know."

"Thanks," I said. "Love and lose, love and win, dust yourself off and love again."

"Amen," he said.

Before I left, Father Peter made me promise to get him Corey Magorey's autograph so he could frame it for his wall.

Chapter Twenty

- Lucky Break -

"Even a blind squirrel finds a nut once in awhile." — *Unknown*

There isn't anything in the world that prepares you for the death of a loved one, yet you can't just give up on the rest of your life, either. I had to find a way to move on. I would have to do the same thing when Steven left the world. That's life, and there isn't any way around it.

I wasn't ready to find any answers in the life of Corey Magorey, but his life inspired me to move forward. The University of Connecticut marched through the NCAA tournament as the highest-seeded team. Corey was by far and away the best player in the country. I was the only reporter with access to him.

On March twenty-seventh, with the entire nation watching, Corey Magorey cut down the nets at Madison Square Garden. He scored thirty-three points in the championship game as Connecticut whipped Kentucky. As the national media converged on Corey, he found me at center court. He placed the net over my head and wrapped a huge arm around my shoulder. The camera lights were blinding. The crowd noise was deafening, and it dawned on me that my face was being transmitted across the nation. CBS Sports' number one announcer met us at half-court.

"How's it feel to win the championship?" the reporter answered.

"It's awesome!" Corey shouted. "I need to thank my mother and this man right here."

The announcer glanced at me for a split-second, but obviously I wasn't the focal point.

"Right now, you're projected as the number one pick. Will you be declaring for the NBA draft? Or will you return to school for your senior year?"

Corey hesitated, looking to me for the answer. We had discussed the idea of playing professional basketball, but I had lobbied hard for his return to school.

"Whatever decision I make depends on what we decide together. I wouldn't be here if it weren't for Leo Brown. Anyone looking to sign me will have to deal with him."

The reporter's eyes lit up with the idea of scooping the competition.

"So, Leo Brown, what will it be?"

It was a moment I waited for my entire life. I was the envy of every reporter in the nation. I had the world's biggest star, on the world's biggest stage, deferring to me. I had millions of people waiting on my every word.

"Will he turn pro?" the reporter asked again.

"Geez, I don't know," I answered.

Corey led me away from the CBS camera and we exploded into laughter. We were just enjoying the moment and the world would have to wait for our decision.

◊ ◊ ◊

A couple of hours later, I walked with Corey through the streets of New York. We couldn't make it more than a few steps before being approached by adoring fans or a reporter looking for a story.

"You're the toast of the town," I said.

I knew that he was satisfied, but he seemed more at peace with the world than I had ever seen him.

"I dreamed of all this," he said. "Yet, deep down, I'm not sure I ever expected it to come true."

"I know what you mean," I said.

"Thanks for making me believe in myself," Corey said.

He draped an arm around my shoulder. I knew that his desire to excel had very little to do with me.

"You pointed me in the right direction," he said.

I wasn't sure where we were walking. I knew we weren't far from the Garden, or the party erupting inside.

"Keep your head on straight," I said. "Don't let it get out of hand tonight."

"Man, I'm beyond that," Corey answered. "But where do you think you're going?"

"I'm heading back to Connecticut," I said.

"Why don't you stay?" Corey asked. "We just won the national championship."

"I need to straighten my own life out. I haven't even seen Amy. We've been through so much in the past few months. We need to get back to what was right between us."

Corey extended his hand, and I shook it for all that I was worth.

"You're a good man," he said.

Somehow, I was going to have to figure out a way to believe him.

◊ ◊ ◊

Amy was sitting at the kitchen table, reading an account of last night's game. The steam rose off her coffee and her hair was still wet from the shower.

"I saw you on television," she said.

"I did great, huh?"

She offered a half-smile, and it was my first clue that we were on the verge of a powerful discussion. I leaned in and kissed her in an attempt to avoid the talk.

"It must have been incredible to be there," she said.

I sat across from her. She dropped her eyes to the newspaper.

"You know, after all I've been through, it wasn't as amazing as I thought it would be. The media and the fans were absolutely crazy, and it was exciting being around the team, but when it's all said and done, it's just a game."

She looked up, and I saw hope in her eyes.

"Where are we going?" she asked.

I had no idea how I was supposed to answer that question.

"Are we going to spend our lives together?" she asked.

I sighed heavily, and moved to the coffee pot. I didn't feel like going into it because I honestly didn't know the answer.

"Of course," I said. It was an automatic response and she knew it.

"I don't want to put pressure on you, but really, Leo, where are we going?"

We'd been together for over three years, and we weren't all that far from where we started. Yet, you get used to anything, and sooner or later it becomes your life.

"Can't we just be together?" I asked.

I sat down, and she stood up. She rinsed her cup in the sink.

"Are we together?" she asked.

It was one of those rhetorical questions that I'm not very good at answering. She rifled around in the drawer next to the refrigerator and produced a letter from my mother.

"Your father left you some money."

She pushed the envelope across the table towards me.

"I felt guilty opening it and I think that's a shame. I pretended like I had a right to know, but lately it feels like I'm intruding in on your life."

It was the crux of the matter, and although I was aggravated by the fact that she had opened the letter, I couldn't let it show. I glanced at the note from Dad's lawyer. My father had left forty thousand dollars. He had setup a trust fund that allowed me to collect most of the money without being buried by taxes. It was money I could have lived without. I would've rather had my Dad.

"It's okay you opened it," I whispered. "You're a huge part of my life."

Her back was to me, and I watched her shoulders sag.

"I don't want to push you," she said.

I wasn't exactly sure what she needed me to say, and I wasn't certain that I could say it. She let the moment pass and re-joined me at the table.

"Maybe it's because we aren't that young anymore," Amy said. "I was talking to my mother about it. She thinks it's time we move forward."

"Good for your mother," I said. "I don't know what's going on right now. Corey wants me to work with him. That could be worth a lot of money. Besides, Steven's sick, and I plan on spending time in Buffalo. I know you don't want to hear it, but what happens to Claire and Steven matters to me."

She rested her chin in the palm of her right hand.

"Back to the original question," she said. "Where are *we* going?"

For most of my adult life, she had stood beside me. She had never asked me for anything more than my attention. Deep down, I knew that she wasn't asking any more than that from me now. I had spent every moment of our life together trying to drift away from her, but she just hadn't let me go.

"I don't know why you want to be lonely," she said. "I just can't figure it out."

I couldn't answer her. Long after she had left the table and closed the bedroom door on me, I sat contemplating her final words on the subject. What was I trying to accomplish by keeping her at arm's length?

◊ ◊ ◊

The weeks following Connecticut's championship flew by in a whirl-wind of speculation and inquiries. I spent a great number of evenings in seclusion with Corey Magorey and his immediate family in a search for direction. If Magorey declared himself eligible for the professional basket-ball draft, there was a better then even chance that he could end up with the Boston Celtics, as they owned two of the seven lottery picks.

On April 15th, Corey Magorey made the decision of a lifetime. The cameras flashed all around us as we stood at the podium. Magorey announced that he was foregoing his final year at Connecticut and declaring himself eligible for the draft. Two days later, we got the call that would change our lives.

Paul Norman, the general manager of the Boston Celtics, contacted me to discuss Corey's future.

"If we hit the lottery, we intend to make Corey the number one pick in the draft," Norman said.

I stifled my glee and thanked him for his consideration.

"The only thing standing in the way of us making that selection is a long, drawn-out salary negotiation. Do you think we can get a deal done?"

It was a question I had no business answering. I was representing Magorey in the most crucial decision of his life. I wasn't a lawyer or a sports agent. I didn't have any basis on which to answer such a question. Yet, I trusted my relationship with Corey enough to know that I could speak for him.

"I'm sure we could work something out," I said.

As I hung up the telephone, the gravity of the situation smacked me squarely between the eyes. I had believed in Corey enough to make a commitment of epic proportions. It was something that I couldn't do for Amy.

◊ ◊ ◊

In the spring, my life moved along rather routinely. Steven was in and out of the hospital for tests, but he appeared to be in great spirits. Claire was excited by her pregnancy, and each conversation seemed to turn into a discussion of names for the unborn child.

My life with Amy remained stagnant. We played house as a husband and wife that had long grown weary of one another. On the good days, we'd share dinner and recount our days. On the tough days, we'd watch television in separate rooms as we considered our future.

The talks with the Celtics continued to heat up. The NBA draft wasn't scheduled until the summer, but the Celtics appeared to be thrilled with the background check into Corey's life. They particularly liked the way that he carried himself after I came into his life. My future took a clear turn with one telephone call. The Celtics general manager, Paul Norman, helped make a few decisions for me.

"How's Corey doing?" he asked.

"He's staying in shape," I said. "The media's on him, but he's trying to be a regular college student."

"That's good. Real good, in fact."

It sounded as though there were more on Norman's mind.

"How's your career?" he asked.

"Great," I said. "Why, what's up?"

"I have something for you to consider," Norman said. "Do you know the Celtics tradition?"

"I know everything about the team," I said. "I've watched Cousy and Russell on the old films. Bird and McHale were like gods to me."

Norman paused for effect. He had my interest and he was about to drive it home.

"How'd you like to meet those guys?" he asked.

I remembered that I was a professional reporter. I shouldn't have reacted in such an excited manner, but I couldn't control myself.

"Are you fucking kidding me?" I asked.

Norman laughed boisterously.

"There's an alumni dinner later in the month; we'd like for you to come."

It was an obvious no-brainer. I smiled into the receiver.

"Better yet, how would you like to join the Celtics family?"

I had been standing, but now I fell into the easy chair.

"You can't be serious," I said. "Guys like me don't get to work for the Celtics."

"Let me tell you what we're thinking. You'd be around full-time to work with Corey, and you'd also become a part of our public relations staff. We know you're a sportswriter. We'll get you a column, whatever you want."

I was too stunned to speak.

"We realize you have a fine position with your paper, but we'd make it financially attractive to you," Norman said. "Why don't you think about it?"

It was important for me to hold onto a bit of dignity. I couldn't just accept the offer without considering it at length.

"Here's the idea," Norman said. "We'll fly you in for the alumni dinner. You can bring a guest, of course, but it can't be Corey. We don't want to be accused of tampering. Before the dinner, we can have a little chat about the position."

"I'll be waiting for the tickets," I said.

I hung up the telephone and stared at it as though I had imagined the news that it had sent me. I thought of the chance to shake Larry Bird's hand. I considered inviting Claire, but all at once it hit me. Steven would love to go along. I never actually thought of taking Amy.

◊   ◊   ◊

Later that night, I was in my home office working on a column for the following week. I was just starting to find that old writing groove when Amy tapped on the door. Aggravated by the interruption, I leaned back in my chair. I still hadn't told her of the Celtics offer because I hadn't yet worked it out in my mind.

"What is it?" I asked.

She had a nervous look on her face. She sort of half-smiled and pulled her hands from behind her back to produce brochures of some sort.

"I've got an idea," she said. "We need a vacation."

There were a couple of brochures detailing a cruise, and a public relations pamphlet from Bermuda. I glanced at them quickly.

"What do you think?" she asked.

She stood in the doorway as though she were afraid to come in. I knew that I owed her at least an answer, so I studied the Bermuda pamphlet a little closer.

"I'd love to go," I said. "But I don't know when."

She took a couple of steps towards me. Her smile was infectious. I realized that she probably had already set it up in her head.

"We can fly for two hundred bucks, round-trip. I looked into a couple of hotels and they aren't real bad. It was eighty-eight there today."

She was just inches from me. I didn't want to completely dash her hopes, but what could I do?

"I heard from the Celtics today," I said.

Her smile dimmed.

"They want to talk to me about a full-time job. They invited me to an alumni dinner later this month, and I figure I'll take Steven along. If I take the job, I'll have to move up there. It's a long way off, but we have to think about it."

The color drained from her face. She took a step backwards, but leaned in to pick up the brochures.

"When were you going to tell me this?" she asked.

"I just got the call," I said.

"I can't just up and move, you know," she said.

She retreated to her spot in the doorway. The magnitude of it all came crashing down on her head.

"Do you even want me to go?" she asked.

I leaned my head back and closed my eyes.

"That's what we have to talk about."

Tears raced down her cheeks. I hadn't meant to upset her, but I clearly understood why she felt left out in the cold.

"No," she sobbed. "That wasn't the question. Do you want me to go?"

I shook my head as though she was being absolutely ridiculous.

"Of course, I want you to go," I said.

She stepped from the room and turned her back on me.

"It doesn't sound like I was part of the plan," she said. "You're taking Steven to the interview. "

"I didn't even call Steven yet," I said.

The sound of her cries was too much to bear. I moved to her, but she didn't want any part of it.

"Leave me alone," she said. "Just leave me the fuck alone."

"Come on," I said.

"No! Why don't you just take Claire? You're just waiting for Steven to die so you can go after her, anyway."

The thought of it infuriated me. She was behind the couch and I was in front of it. No matter which way I moved, she went in the other direction. We were like a brother and sister in the middle of a huge fight.

"I can't believe you'd even think that," I said.

She was sobbing uncontrollably, but she still wouldn't let me get close.

"Don't you see?" she asked.

"See what?" I asked.

"Don't you see that no one is ever going to love you like I do?"

She broke around the edge of the couch and raced for the front door. She was down the front steps and out into the street in a flash. I heard her crying as she ran. Hands down, it was the lowest moment of my life. I didn't chase her.

The next day, I returned home from work not knowing what to expect. I wanted her to be there, but something inside me said that maybe it would be best if she left. Maybe we had truly loved and lost. I turned the doorknob, afraid to enter my own home.

I didn't see her at first, and it didn't appear that life was any different. She hadn't loaded the furniture in a van and taken off on me. But she did come out of the bedroom with a cardboard box filled with clothes.

"Can we talk?" I asked.

She smiled, and I was surprised at the way it made me feel. She was everything a man could ask for in a woman.

"Leo, let's just let it go, all right?"

"Come on, Amy."

She stockpiled boxes by the door. I sat on the couch and watched her. If she was going to walk away, I wasn't going to help her. Yet, I had been the one to push her to the door.

"Today I was thinking about all the relationships that end," she said. "In every one of those relationships, there's a last time that you make love. There's a last time that you feel comfortable in each other's arms."

She glanced at me as though she had let me in on the secret of life.

"I don't know what the hell you're talking about," I said.

"It's over, Leo. I'm done. Good luck, good night and goodbye. I have to go."

I would have argued with her, but she didn't let me. She took two boxes down to her car. I kept waiting for her to return for the rest of her stuff, but she must have figured she could make do without it. It dawned on me that she was trying to ask me where my love had gone.

"We all make decisions," I said to the four walls surrounding me. "She just made a huge one, for both of us."

For the next six weeks, I wallowed in self-pity.

◊ ◊ ◊

In early May, I flew into Buffalo and drove to Claire and Steven's house. As it turns out, I wasn't ready for the way that either of them looked.

Claire was in her sixth month of pregnancy. I don't know what made me expect to see her perfect body, but, of course, it wasn't there.

"I've gained fourteen pounds," she said. "Isn't it wonderful?"

She twirled around a couple of times, and I laughed before hugging her to me.

152

I stared at her for a long time. Most of it was because I didn't want to look at Steven. His eyes and skin had turned slightly yellow. While he had looked sickly at my mother's wedding, now he looked like a corpse.

"So we're meeting Larry Bird, huh?"

We shook hands, and I pulled him into a hug.

"Bird, McHale, Cousy, maybe even Havlicek," I said. When I looked into his eyes, I knew I had made the right choice about who to take to Boston.

Claire went to the kitchen and returned with a couple of sodas.

"We have a few minutes to visit, don't we?" she asked.

I checked my watch. I thought of all the afternoons we had spent together. We had never cared about time. Now, we were fighting for just a few more moments.

"Yeah, sure, we have a couple of hours," I said.

"So, how's Amy?" Claire asked.

It wasn't how I would have started the discussion.

◊   ◊   ◊

Claire wasn't pleased with me. In fact, it took all of my strength to stop her from calling Amy. She sat across from me, scolding me with her eyes.

"Something just wasn't right," I said. "It never was." Claire wasn't buying it.

"You know what love is?" she asked.

I half-shrugged.

"It's being there for one another. It's taking care of each other when things aren't perfect. It's holding one another when you're scared. It's laughing together when you're happy."

"It wasn't Camelot," I said.

Claire stole a glance at Steven.

"Do you think this is Camelot?" Steven asked.

I couldn't imagine their love being anything but perfect.

"I have cancer that will probably kill me. Do you see Claire walking away? I'm not exactly the perfect human specimen anymore."

I didn't want to talk about Amy anymore. At that point, I would have rather discussed the cancer.

"Do they know how you got it?" I asked.

Steven chuckled.

"They say it was caused by inherited abnormalities." He sat down beside Claire.

"Isn't that a kick in the balls?" he said. "There never was anything I could do to stop it. I had it when I was born. Now, I have, at the most, six months to live."

He laughed for some reason.

"I never knew I'd learn so much about my freaking liver," he said. He stood and took a bow. "The liver creates, regulates, and stores a variety of substances used by the gastrointestinal system. During a meal, bile is secreted by liver cells and travels through the hepatic duct system into the small intestine where it is used to break down fat molecules." I looked at Claire. She shrugged her shoulders and smiled.

"The liver plays a role in the regulation of blood sugar. It synthesizes, dissolves, and stores amino acids, protein and fat. It stores vitamins and disposes of cellular waste and alcohol."

"I don't even know what that means," I said.

"Me neither," Steven said.

This time, we all laughed.

"The bottom line is that I got a bum liver from the manufacturer and I must have missed the recall notice."

He sat between us again.

"How do you live with what's going to happen?" I asked.

"What else am I going to do? I want to live long enough to see the baby." He rested his hand on Claire's stomach. "When I die, I want to make sure that all I have left to do is die."

"That's all anyone can ask," I said.

His symptoms were relatively mild, but he had completely lost his appetite.

"I have to force food down him," Claire said.

There was a gradual loss of sensory power, and his limbs felt weak all through the day. He usually slept thirteen hours, but he made the most of his time when awake.

"How are you guys with money?" I asked.

"Claire has tremendous medical insurance so we're all right there," Steven said.

"But there are times when I'm sitting at work thinking only of him," Claire said. "Every minute I spend away from him is a lost minute. I'm going to take leave in a few weeks. We'll bring in the baby together."

Neither appeared on the edge of tears. It was the greatest display of bravery that I had ever seen.

"Are they treating you?" I asked.

I looked away from them long enough to pick up the soda. I took a quick gulp to remove the lump I felt in my throat.

"They put a needle into the tumor every now and then. They call it x-ray treatment. It lasts about ten minutes. I'm out of the hospital in four hours or so."

"Is it helping you?" I asked.

Steven stood again and spread his arms wide.

"You be the judge. How do I look?"

I smiled as Steven twirled in front of me.

"I was such a good athlete," he said. "I could run like a deer, jump like a rabbit, and stop myself on a dime. I was slamming a basketball at seventeen. I made the state all-star team. I won most valuable in soccer, baseball, and basketball. I thought it meant everything. In the end, it doesn't mean shit."

I bowed my head. It was almost too much to take. I felt the now familiar pain of loss as I considered Weird Henry and Dad.

"Don't feel sorry for us," he said. "We'll meet up again, and every day will be like those long summer days when we were kids."

"I hope you're right," I said.

Even if they weren't going to cry, I couldn't control it.

"Leo, the thing is, you have to take everything life has to offer," Claire said. "There's so much that we don't know about any of this. We didn't do anything to deserve this, but it might be to our advantage to handle it the right way."

Suddenly, meeting Larry Bird didn't seem so important. The idea that they could smile through the pain was beyond comprehension.

"Would you please call Amy?" Claire asked.

"You know, I still don't know anything about anything," I said.

"Just consider what's important," Claire said.

It was hard to argue with them. I bowed my head to the floor.

Chapter Twenty-One

– I'm Free –

"The happiest time in any man's life is after the first divorce."
— *John Kenneth Galbraith*

Steven's façade of bravery came crumbling down as soon as we got into the car. I had to practically lift him into the passenger seat. When I slipped in behind the wheel and turned to face him, the tears racing down his face sent a wave of sheer panic through my body.

"What's going to happen to Claire?" he asked. "I keep imagining her life without me, and it scares the shit out of me."

"She'll be okay," I said.

I made a move to start the engine, but Steven grabbed my arm.

"Just say that she lives to be eighty," he said. "When it's all said and done, I would have been in her life for just over a quarter of it. How will she ever remember me?"

I needed a little of Claire's wisdom to comfort Steven. I pressed my eyes closed and silently prayed that I'd say the right thing.

"If she makes it to eighty," I said, "you'll have been with her eighty years. You've given her a child. You've had enough love to last a lifetime. Every time she sees that child, she'll be reminded of you."

He allowed my hand to break free from his tender grasp.

"It still sucks," he said.

"Big time."

I leaned across the seat and pulled him into a hug.

"Do me a favor," Steven said. "Marry her after I'm gone."

I couldn't have answered him if I wanted to. I felt his body shake under my embrace. It was too much for a man to take.

"Please," he said.

"I'll do my best to make sure she's okay," I said.

The mood lightened a bit as the airplane pierced the clouds. Steven settled back into his seat and slipped off to sleep. I watched him for a few moments, realizing that the real world couldn't get to him when he was asleep. It was so hard to fathom that he would be dead in just a short time. I wondered about Weird Henry and my father. Where were they now? Were they looking down at me, laughing about my lack of wisdom? Did they know that Steven would be a lot better off in a few months time? Or were they simply gone forever?

I flipped through the pages of the in-flight magazine, but my mind drifted to thoughts of Amy. We had developed a true love, and I had done everything in my power to break it down. Had I really intended to make it fail? Was I still thinking of Claire?

I fell into a daydream of the future. Steven would pass away, and I would help Claire through the grieving. We would support one another as we had all those years ago. Our love would flourish, and together we would raise their child.

I leaned back against the seat. The airplane hummed along, and Steven softly snored beside me. I closed my eyes on the daydream, understanding that through all of the years, I was still trying to fool myself. Life wasn't what I imagined it to be. Yet, the living of life was in the journey, and not the final destination.

◊ ◊ ◊

The one thing that truly escapes you when you're imagining meeting your childhood heroes is that they are just mere mortals. I spent most of the evening with an eye on Larry Bird and Kevin McHale. I watched as they ate their dinners and chatted with their comrades. Bird appeared to have a bit of a cold, and it blew my mind to understand that he suffered from the same afflictions as the rest of us.

Paul Norman was in and out of the room. He worked the crowd like a used car salesman. He gave us the red carpet treatment, and while my mood was a bit subdued, Steven seemed to be having the time of his life. There wasn't a single Celtic there who didn't shake his hand, and when word of his cancer made its rounds, Steven was lavished with gifts. Bird and McHale posed for a photo with him. Bob Cousy signed a basketball, and the current Celtics presented courtside tickets for a game against the Lakers. Steven glanced down at the date on the tickets.

"I probably won't be here in December," he whispered.

We didn't spend a lot of time at the party after dinner. Although Steven pretended that everything was fine, his eyes told the story. There were actually moments when I thought he'd fall right out of his chair.

We hailed a taxi and headed for the Holiday Inn. Steven had a cardboard box filled with souvenirs, and I had a promise of a three-year personal services contract, if and when Magorey signed on the dotted line.

"It was awesome," Steven said. "Thank you."

I helped him into bed as though he were an infant child. I pulled the covers up around his neck and sat on the edge of the bed.

"You know," he said, "we met some great men today. Those guys played basketball better than anyone else in the world."

"They were something else," I said.

His eyes were closed, and I was sure that he'd be sleeping in a matter of seconds.

"But, when it's all said and done, it don't mean shit."

He struggled for a breath, and all at once, started laughing. His eyes remained pressed closed.

"I shook Larry Bird's hand tonight. He put his arm around my shoulder and whispered, 'Hang in there.'"

Steven continued laughing. He went on for so long that I wondered if he hadn't simply lost his mind.

"When we were in high school, I was the king shit, you know? Everyone wanted to be my friend. I had the best girl. I was the best athlete. Man, I was voted most likely to succeed."

"You've had a wonderful life," I said.

"And it didn't mean shit," he said. "They should've voted me most likely to succumb."

It was more than I could take. I edged away from the bed as the tears started to fall.

"Thanks for being my friend, man."

"It's not a sacrifice," I said. I barely choked out the words. Part of me wished that he'd just go to sleep. In my heart though, I didn't want the night to ever end.

"You know," he said, "if God gave me the choice…"

He struggled to sit upright. I rushed to him, and slowly brought him forward.

"If God told me that I'd live a short life and have a slow, agonizing death, I'd still do it. Do you know why?"

I shook my head.

"Why?" I asked.

"Because he gave me you and Claire."

He sobbed, and I buried my head in his chest.

"I love you," he said.

For the rest of my days, I'd regret not being able to answer him. I just couldn't find my voice. I held him in my arms and sobbed. He drifted off to sleep in that position, and I lowered him back onto the bed. I softly touched the side of his cheek. I leaned in and kissed him on the forehead.

◊ ◊ ◊

The next day, we flew back to Buffalo. For most of the trip, it was like having old Steven back. We laughed at the people rushing through the airport.

"The airport terminal is the best place to watch people," Steven said. "They're in their most stripped down, vulnerable state."

He pointed to a businessman with a briefcase.

"That guy thinks he's the king of the world," he said. "He feels so important because he's flying and the company's paying for it. He's probably got a girlfriend in every city. He thinks he's entitled to fly first-class, and he looks down his nose at everyone in his path."

159

Almost on cue, the businessman began screaming at the lady behind the ticket-counter.

"You see, grade-one asshole," Steven said. "And then there's that guy."

Steven pointed to a man carrying a tattered, old suitcase. The man's face was a portrait of despair.

"He's the kind of guy who's flying because that's what he has to do. He probably has three kids at home that depend on him to go to work. He probably cried on the way to the airport, wishing he could stay home a little longer."

Sure enough, the man tapped me on the shoulder and asked for directions to the pay phones.

"I told my kids I'd call before the airplane took off," the man said.

Steven had a smug look on his face. I couldn't help but smile.

"You know what the best part of dying is?" Steven asked.

I shook my head.

"You see everything crystal clear," he said. "Right now, I can see through all of the charades. I've broken down what's important and what isn't, and truthfully, all of this is kind of comical."

I thought of my father, and the letter he left behind. He said he'd been able to take stock of his life and figure out what had been truly important. In a lot of ways, even Weird Henry had been able to sift through the muck.

"I feel sorry for the people who don't get the chance to get it all straight," Steven said.

I didn't want to mention he was sitting beside one such fellow.

"Yeah, that's a shame," I said.

◊ ◊ ◊

While I was in Buffalo, Amy had returned to clean out the rest of her stuff from the apartment. It was unbelievable how empty I felt inside. I walked from room to room, assessing the bare walls. I looked everywhere for a reminder of our life together, but she had removed every trace of our relationship.

For the first time in nearly four years, I was completely alone. More than anything else, I needed some company. I called Corey to tell him about the alumni dinner, but he wasn't home, and his answering machine cut me off halfway through my message.

"That's all right," I said. "I can make this work."

The sound of my voice in the empty room sounded a bit strange. "I'll make it work."

I took a notepad and flopped down on the couch. I had every intention of jotting down my thoughts for the future. I was looking to define where I was going and what I still wanted out of life.

I wrote "Boston Celtics" across the top of the paper, and couldn't think of anything else to write. Why was I following Corey Magorey to Boston? What if the Celtics didn't get the first pick in the draft? Was it more of the same old thing? Was I hanging my hat on a dream that just wouldn't come true?

I dialed the operator and asked for a listing for Amy Moran.

"I'm sorry," the operator said.

"Are you sure?" I asked. "She just moved."

"What town is she living in?" the operator asked.

I imagined the annoyed look on the operator's face.

"Can you check New Haven, West Haven, and East Haven?"

"I'm sorry, sir. I don't have all day to chase down this girl for you."

"It's okay," I said. "Really, it's all right."

"Maybe you should have talked to her before she left," the anonymous lady answered.

She clicked the line dead. I sat there for a long time, staring at the telephone in my hand. I fought off the urge to call Claire.

Chapter Twenty-Two

– Back in time –

"I've just learned about his illness. Let's hope it's nothing trivial."
— Variously Ascribed

The Celtics chose Corey with the first pick in the draft, and I signed a personal services contract for three years. In short, it worked out just as I had imagined. I tied up the loose ends in Connecticut, and at the end of June, I walked out of my apartment for the very last time. I worked my schedule so that there'd be a week between the end of my New Haven life and the start of my life in Boston.

The hours before I left were spent in bars across the state of Connecticut. I wasn't interested in drinking. Pure and simple, I was searching for Amy. I didn't find her.

I drove to Boston with a perpetual ache in my heart. For one reason or another, I couldn't get that old saying, about how if you loved something you had to set it free, out of my head. Was love just a game that was dependent upon luck and fate? Perhaps I *was* supposed to wind up with Claire. In any regard, I needed to find the answers.

The Celtics found me a home on the outskirts of Boston. It was a neat little apartment that actually mirrored what I had in Connecticut. I spent the first four hours of my new life unpacking. The team had arranged for the hook-up of all my utilities, and when I was through unpacking, I turned on *SportsCenter* and called Steven. I had officially taken my pitiful life on the road.

◊ ◊ ◊

In early July, I attended a press conference as a Celtics team official. Corey Magorey had agreed to a four-year contract worth a little less than seventeen million dollars. As Paul Norman briefed the media on the signing, I stood in a back room with Corey at my side.

"Can you believe this?" he asked.

"It's an incredible amount of money," I said. "You deserve it. You've worked for it."

Corey laughed hard.

"I don't deserve this. No man deserves this."

In a matter of moments, he was to be introduced as the savior of the Celtics. If his career were anything like he imagined, he would be forever linked to Larry Bird and the rest of the Celtic greats.

"There's a price to pay," I said. "That money comes with responsibility. You have to be dynamic on the court, fair to the media, a role model to the fans, and true to yourself."

Again, Corey laughed.

"True to myself," he said. "That's a hot one coming from you."

Paul Norman finished the introduction. Corey climbed the stage and Norman outfitted him with a Celtics cap. The reporters shouted their questions and, with the patience of a saint, Corey answered them. Before leaving the podium, Corey turned to face me.

"I have to thank Leo Brown," Corey said. "If he hadn't taught me about reality, I would've been in a jail somewhere. Thanks, Leo. We'll figure it out, right?"

That night, I punched out the press release detailing Magorey's signing. I spent precious little time talking about his exploits on the court. Instead, I extolled the virtues of his newfound faith in life.

Something clicked inside of me. I would take it day-by-day. I would be true to myself, and it would work out in the end. Maybe I didn't deserve a happy ending, but Corey didn't deserve seventeen million dollars, and Steven didn't deserve cancer.

I scribbled down the final paragraph of my press release. The news wires picked up on it and the entire nation read my words of advice to

Corey Magorey. Little did anyone know that it was advice that I had borrowed from Claire after pissing my pants in little league.

Corey, remember that people will look at you as you look at yourself. We all fall flat on our faces now and then. The best part of life is that you always get another chance.

◊   ◊   ◊

On the morning of July tenth, I received the telephone call that I had long dreaded. It wasn't much of a surprise, as Claire and I discussed Steven's deteriorating condition on a daily basis.

"It's time to go to the hospital," Claire announced.

She was still a week from her due date, so there was no mistaking what she was talking about.

"He's just about hanging on," she said.

There weren't any tears, and her voice didn't betray her.

"I'll be there in a few hours," I said. "How are *you* feeling?"

"I'm facing the start of a life, and the end of a life. I guess I'm kind of busy." She sort of half-laughed, and I wished I was beside her. "Steven's standard joke is that we're both due any day now."

"That's not funny," I said.

"Well, we're handling it. My doctor's going to induce labor so Steven can hold the baby before he dies."

I tried to imagine the scene, but it was too much to handle. I grabbed the bag that I had packed long ago for a trip that I didn't want to make.

◊   ◊   ◊

I took a window seat and watched the world get smaller as the plane moved up into the clouds. The years gone past seemed like one long day. From the first moment of conscious thought to the moment when the airplane pierced the clouds, I had been surviving on hurt and self-pity. My trip home needed to be a celebration of Steven's life. More than likely, he'd be gone before the end of the week.

The man seated in front of me slammed the back of his seat into my knees. I almost reached over the seat to ask him if I could have a little more room, but in the grand scheme of things it hardly seemed to matter. The flight attendant leaned in.

"Do you feel all right?" she asked.

"I'm still alive," I said.

Her face contorted a bit as she tried to figure out what I was saying.

"A glass of water would be nice," I said.

I took my checkbook out of my travel bag. I had transferred the money left to me by my father into my personal account. There were so many people that judged success or failure by the numbers in a bank account. In my case, I was an unmitigated success. I was a young man with over sixty thousand dollars in the bank.

I wrote a check for twenty-five thousand dollars and signed it over to Claire. I wasn't sure how I would get her to take it, but it wasn't nearly enough to cover her losses.

The flight attendant handed me the glass of cold water. The man in front of me moved his seat forward, and I stretched my legs out. The water was ice cold and felt sweet on my tongue.

I'm still alive.

I couldn't get rid of the ache in my heart, but there was so much more of life to live.

◊ ◊ ◊

The staff at Buffalo General Hospital made special arrangements for Claire and Steven. The preparation work was going on all around me, and I felt like a bit actor in a bad movie. Claire was on her feet, orchestrating the maneuvers. I stood off to the side, peering down at Steven in his deathbed and listening to the worried ramblings of Claire's mother.

Steven's condition wasn't good and from all indications, it was worsening by the minute. He was sleeping peacefully when I arrived, and I sat on his bed watching his chest expand as he struggled to keep breathing.

It was a little after seven in the evening when we were called into a grieving room. Doctor Bogner, who was watching over Steven, and Doctor Lynda Hewitt, who would be delivering the baby, brought us together to explain the procedures.

I held Claire's hand as we sat before the doctors. Claire's mother was due to arrive at any moment, but Claire decided against waiting for her.

"She doesn't want to hear the gruesome details anyway."

Bogner took the floor first.

"I'm sure you want total honesty," he said.

We nodded. I'm not really sure if anyone every truly wanted to be lied to, but I dismissed the thought.

"He won't die tonight. He's stable."

Claire sighed heavily and gripped my hand a little tighter.

"Will he pass tomorrow?" Bogner seemed intent on answering his own question. "I don't know. His system's shutting down. I'm not sure, and I can't promise that he will be coherent. You may have your child and he may never fully realize it."

This time, I squeezed Claire's hand.

"If you believe in divine intervention, this would be a good time to ask for it."

Bogner deferred to Hewitt, but before he walked away, I asked the one question that Claire had to be thinking.

"Is he in pain?"

"I'm not the one lying there," Bogner said. "He's as comfortable as someone who's dying can be."

Hewitt didn't allow us time to reflect. She was a pale, skinny woman that, frankly, scared the hell out of me with her direct manner.

"We've done a number of ultrasounds to make sure the baby is developed to the point we can bring him into the world. So far, everything looks good. We've determined that your child is a good weight, and that you're a good risk for this sort of procedure."

Claire was softly crying. I caressed her back, trying to reassure her as a husband might.

"Of course, we would much rather wait, but we do understand. The child is comfortable now, and it will adapt quickly to the outside world."

I could only hope that it adapted quicker than I had.

Hewitt seemed unsure about how much she should tell us. She stammered around the subject for a while, and Claire brought her back to the matter at hand.

"Is the labor more painful when you induce?" Claire asked. "I'm not much worried about the pain, but I want to know what to expect."

"I understand," Hewitt said. She offered a half-smile that looked funny on her normally placid face. "None of it is much fun without pain-killers. We'll be giving you an IV to administer a drug called pitocin. In some cases, too much pitocin is administered and the contractions can be very strong, and they may come at a fast rate. We'll have your nurse watching this very closely."

"The timing is the important thing," Claire said. "When will we get started?"

"We'll start the induction early tomorrow. By then, you will have been prepped and we'll break your water. About an hour and a half after we start, you'll be given the IV, and you'll begin to feel the contractions anywhere between fifteen minutes and an hour after the pitocin is given. How it goes after that will depend upon you and the baby. It may take some time."

Hewitt asked for additional questions, but I couldn't think of anything, and Claire seemed too overwhelmed to speak.

"Very well then. Try to rest tonight," Hewitt said. She patted Claire's arm, and nodded to me.

"Let's go get something to drink," Claire said.

If she was being brave for me, I truly appreciated it.

The cafeteria was quiet. There was a family gathered in a far corner of the room and although they appeared to be eating their dinner together, they were anything but normal. A middle-aged woman clung to her husband's arm. Together they wailed into their napkins as a teenage girl looked on. Within minutes, we were able to hear most of their story.

Greg was the teenage son, and the brother to the young girl. He wasn't a very experienced driver, and in the end, it did him in. A slick rain turned the driving conditions against him, and he struck a telephone pole that cut his car in half. He was existing with the aid of a respirator, but the doctors didn't hold out much hope.

"It's so depressing," I whispered.

Claire sipped a caffeine-free soda, and I worked on an unsweetened iced tea.

"We don't get any guarantees," I said. "It can all end in a moment."

Claire seemed a bit annoyed with the way the conversation was going.

Clifford Fazzolari

"It's life," she said. Her eyes seemed distant. "I don't mean to be cold, but these things *do* happen. We have to believe there's more for us. If I didn't have the faith, I'd be in a loony bin right now. Someone once told me that the universe takes care of us. I'm clinging to that hope."

Through it all, she smiled. In that smile, I saw everything that she'd been trying to tell me through all of our years together. I saw God actually alive in her eyes.

"Michael's coming in, isn't he?" she asked. She pushed her drink to the center of the table. Greg's mother wailed loudly from the table behind us. "Why don't you spend a little time with him?"

"I want to stay with you," I said.

Claire bowed her head, and when she lifted her eyes, the tears glistened.

"I'm pretty sure this will be Steven and mine's last night together," she said. "I want to be alone with Steven. I hope you understand."

◊ ◊ ◊

I left the hospital after stopping in to say goodbye to Steven. He was still completely incoherent, and my visit left me feeling sad and completely empty. As I was leaving the room, Doctor Bogner wrapped an arm around my shoulder and directed me into the hallway. He handed me an envelope of papers.

"You probably have a few questions on why your buddy is dying," Bogner said.

I shrugged my shoulders as if my questions didn't really matter all that much.

"I gathered some information for you. I understand it won't offer much comfort, but technically, there are reasons why he was untreatable."

I took the envelope from him. His intelligence and compassion were evident, and I couldn't even figure out why. I realized he probably had toenails that were smarter than me.

"How have they been?" I asked.

He looked a bit confused, but all at once, it seemed as though a light bulb went on over his head.

"Steven and Claire are remarkable people," he said. "From day one, they handled it better than any other patients I ever had. They didn't walk around looking for someone to blame. They faced it. Steven fought it as hard as his body would allow, and Claire — let's just say that Claire is somehow above the rest of us."

Bogner patted me on the shoulder.

"I hope you find some solace in all of it. Let me know if there's anything I can do."

I thought about the check in my pocket. I wondered if Bogner could help me pass it along to Claire, but I quickly dismissed the idea.

"Thank you for everything," I said.

He moved down the hall to the next patient. For every one that he lost, I hoped that there were a hundred he'd save.

"You're a better man than me," I whispered to his disappearing form.

I drove around town. I wasn't even sure of the day of the week, but traffic on the thruway was light. Bogner had given me a packet of information on how the cancer affected Steven's liver, and the eventual ruins it left behind.

I parked across the street from Steven's old home. I'm not sure what brought me back to the old neighborhood time and again, but it seemed like the best possible place to visit.

What would eventually kill Steven was something called metastatic liver cancer. The metastatic tumor cells had infected easily accessible areas. The liver, because it acted as a filter, was an integral part of blood circulation. In simple terms, Steven's liver had filtered the cancer to other parts of his body. Chemotherapy was the only viable option, but when it all came down, it was a losing proposition.

I crumpled the papers into a ball. I didn't want any more information about his death. I just wanted to celebrate his life.

I made the short drive to my dead father's house. Michael's car was already in the drive. Inexplicably, so was Amy's.

A solitary light shone from my father's house. I thought of Margaret, and how happy she had been when they moved into the new home. I could almost hear her saying that she felt Dad was hers. Now, she was left to wander the empty rooms looking for something to blame.

I entered quietly, but just as I set foot in the doorway, an explosion of laughter stalled me in my tracks. Michael, Margaret, Amy, and an unidentified man were seated around the kitchen table. They were all looking at Michael, who was drinking beer and telling stories. Margaret saw me first.

"Speak of the devil," she said.

I went straight to the refrigerator and grabbed a beer.

"Anyone else?" I asked.

The unidentified man asked for one.

"So, what kind of shit is Michael feeding you now?" I asked.

Again, only the unidentified man spoke.

"We were just talking about you and your first exposure to the naked form of a woman."

Instantly, I went back in time to the woods behind Halley Road where Weird Henry's girl had done the strip show. I might have smiled if it hadn't suddenly dawned on me that the man was with Amy.

"Who are you?" I asked.

Amy spoke up. They were her first words to me since she ran from our apartment.

"Leo, this is Ken."

My heart sunk as my head filled with questions. Knowing his name didn't really answer my questions. It wasn't the time or place to open up discussions.

"Yeah, good old Weird Henry," I said. "He was always looking out for me. Life was so different back then. Henry acted like he knew everything. Maybe he knew something we don't."

I looked directly at Michael. I took a sip of beer and specifically ignored Amy and Ken.

"I wish I was still that naïve," I said. "I really wish they'd give you some of the information up front, so there aren't so many surprises."

Margaret came around the table, and I stood to hug her. She held on so tightly that I knew her life wasn't anything but lonely.

"I'm sorry about Steven," she said. "You guys are so close."

I felt like crying, but I slugged the beer instead.

"Anyway, we're just telling stories," Michael said. "I'm sure you have one."

All eyes were upon me and I locked in with Amy's. She didn't look away, and immediately I knew that Ken wasn't about to marry her. I don't know what gave it away, but I knew her well enough.

"We used to walk up and down the railroad tracks, across the train trestle and out into the woods. Usually, we were all together. It was Michael, Claire, Steven and myself. Towards the end, Weird Henry came along. Yet, every now and then, you caught yourself alone with just one other person."

I paused long enough to tend to my beer. Ken, noticing that I was already getting low, reciprocated, and brought me another.

"One day after school, Steven and I walked the path alone. We must have been about sixteen," I said.

The room was deathly quiet as they waited on my words. My mind drifted back to that day long ago, and I could almost hear the stones beneath my feet as Steven and I walked along.

"Back in those days, I had a crush on Claire. Did any of you know that I had a thing for Claire?"

There was laughter all around. Amy laughed the loudest.

"This really isn't much of a story, but a single sentence that Steven said to me that day keeps popping into my mind. I guess he was trying to make me feel better. I have a tendency to over think things."

Again, there was laughter, but it was a bit milder as they waited on what Steven had said to me.

"He said, 'Leo, you've got a lot of love in your life. Don't drive yourself crazy by trying to make it the kind of love that you want. Just accept it for what it is.'"

This time, I went back to the refrigerator. I had been inside for less than twenty minutes and I was reaching for my third beer. At this pace, I'd miss the birth, the death, and the funeral.

"Sorry for bringing everyone down," I said. "I just don't feel much like laughing."

I took the beer and moved through the house to the living room. I sat alone in the dark and nursed that third beer for the better part of an hour.

171

Clifford Fazzolari

Amy joined me for a brief moment. She kissed me on the cheek and offered her sympathies.

"We'll all miss Steven," she said. "But, probably you most of all."

I didn't have a suitable response so I just hugged her. The gathering busted up a little while later, and Margaret joined me in the darkness.

"You can stay here," she said.

"I was thinking of going to a hotel," I answered.

She was probably less than ten feet away, but I couldn't even see her.

"I was thinking you could have another beer and sit up with me for a minute. The guest bedroom is all made up and it's just a short walk from here."

In the darkness, our hands met, and I took the beer.

"I miss him so much," she said. "I knew what you were talking about in there about accepting love and not trying to change it. I'm glad I gave your father everything I had, but that don't make it hurt any less."

She might have been crying, but I didn't go to her.

"I know we have to live our lives," she said, "but when I look back at it, it seems like I didn't say 'I love you' enough."

I let a few moments pass. I took a swig of beer, but I didn't really want it.

"You were perfect for Dad," I said.

This time, Margaret let some time go by.

"Amy loves you," she said.

"I know," I answered, "and I'll make it right."

I kissed Margaret on the forehead.

"There's extra pillows and blankets in the closet."

"I remember," I said.

I was halfway down the hall before I turned around.

"Say, Margaret, thanks for being there for Dad," I said.

"It was my pleasure," she said.

This time, I was sure she was crying.

◊ ◊ ◊

The sun shone brightly on the streets of Buffalo, New York. I don't know why, but I kept looking directly at it as though I needed the flash of

172

light it provided. I found the visitors lot and pulled into a spot directly across from the emergency room doors of Buffalo General Hospital.

"Be with me today, God," I said.

The day had hardly started and I was already in tears. I was barely two feet beyond the swing of the doors when my heart made its first leap of the day.

Ethel Campbell had her back to me, and she was hunched down over a walker, but I knew she had come to see Claire through the birth and death. I did all I could to stop myself from hugging the old lady, but in the end, I couldn't resist.

"Leo, right?" she asked.

I punched the elevator button.

"What're you doing here?" I asked.

"I'm here for Claire," she said. "She's called me every day since Anthony passed. I'm just returning the favor."

The idea that Claire kept in contact with Ethel was almost too overwhelming to consider, but it hardly surprised me. The elevator doors opened, and I helped the old woman inside. I hit the button for the maternity ward.

"Don't waste time today imagining how life is going to be down the line," Ethel said.

She extracted her handkerchief and blew her nose quickly.

"It's going to be an unbearable day if you let it be. Just relax and live it."

I leaned in and kissed the old woman on the cheek. The doors sprung open, and she tenderly touched my right cheek.

"Claire and Steven love you exactly as you are. Just be yourself."

We got off the elevator and Ethel stopped in the waiting area beside the information desk.

"You go see her first," she said. "I need to rest for a minute."

There were two nurses in Claire's room prepping her for the day's work. I tried to stay back, out of the way.

"Come here," Claire said.

173

I went to her bedside and leaned in. She wrapped her arms around me. I tried to kiss her cheek, but wound up hitting her neck.

"It'll go good," I said.

The nurses were in and out of the room, but they were virtually invisible to me.

"Have you seen Steven yet?"

"Not yet," I said.

Her face lit up. She brushed away a tear that I hadn't seen.

"You should go down there. He looks really good. They put him directly below me. I wanted him in the same room, but what're you going to do?"

"I'll run back and forth to give him updates," I said.

Claire slid up in bed and adjusted the pillow behind her.

"Actually, I was hoping you'd stay by my side," she said. "A child should be greeted by a mother and a father. I know Steven won't mind if it's your face the baby sees first."

I pulled her into another hug, but she nudged me away.

"Go see Steven. I have about an hour to rest, and I'm waiting for Ethel."

"I love you," I said. I turned away, and headed for the door.

"So I've heard," she said.

I spun back around to see her smile.

"I love you too," she answered.

I couldn't go directly to Steven's room. I went to the lobby and walked around in circles. I grabbed a newspaper, thinking that Steven might actually be interested in how the baseball pennant races were heating up. Finally, I went back up in that elevator, prepared to face it all head-on.

Steven was propped up in bed. He wasn't exactly sitting, but he wasn't flat on his back, either. His drawn face and ashen color were no longer a shock. I walked in wearing my biggest smile.

"Good morning," I said.

"Hey, buddy," he said. "How are you doing?"

I tossed the newspaper on the table beside his bed.

"Did the Yankees win?" he asked.

"Seven to one," I said.

He closed his eyes for a split-second, and I dreaded the idea that he was in pain.

"Sit down," he said.

I pulled the chair close to the bed.

"How's Claire?" he asked.

I couldn't help but laugh.

"She's doing great," I said. "She's worried about you."

"You tell her not to worry, okay? You make sure she doesn't have any trouble today."

"I will."

There wasn't much to look at in the room. Steven was being fed through an IV, but the nurses were simply trying to make him comfortable.

"This is my last day," he said.

I wanted to assure him that he'd have more time, but our friendship took us beyond such a denial.

"Leo," he said, "I ain't going out easy."

He pressed his eyes closed. I sat watching him, hoping he'd just keep talking.

"I don't have any regrets," he said. "Not one. I don't have any guilt in my heart. I always tried to do the right thing."

I needed to take his mind off it, but talking about the Yankees wasn't going to work.

"We're having a baby today. It's like a golden sunrise, you know? We should celebrate birth more."

He opened his eyes, and turned to look directly into mine.

"Make sure my baby comes into a happy world."

"I will," I whispered.

"I'm counting on you, Leo. Go upstairs and make sure it's perfect."

"You have my word," I said. "Just try to relax. I'll bring that baby down to you."

"All right then, get going."

I forced myself to stand up. I wondered if I'd see him alive again.

"I'm going to be here when you get back," he said.

I shuffled towards the door.

"Leo?"

"Yeah?"

"Just in case I'm not, always know that you're right here." He pointed at his heart.

175

Clifford Fazzolari

I all but ran back towards the bed. I hugged him and we cried. It seemed as though we cried for an hour.

◊ ◊ ◊

The next three hours were a whirlwind of emotion. I held ice to Claire's lips in the moments between contractions. I held her hand as she endured the undying stabs of pain. I could only imagine what was happening inside of her, but the words "golden sunrise" kept swimming around in my mind.

We talked of Steven and their days and nights of love and passion. We crossed a line beyond friendship and deep into love. All of the feelings I had for Claire, through all of the years, paled in comparison of her love for Steven. Yet, the love that *we* held for each other was from somewhere out of this world, too.

Every so often, Amy or Michael popped into the room with words of encouragement from Steven. Although they administered the pitocin at eight o'clock, shortly after noon, we were still waiting on the baby's arrival.

"It won't be long now," said one of the nurses.

Dr. Hewitt was in position at the foot of the bed. I wiped sweat away from Claire's brow, and she smiled up at me through closed eyes.

"Are you ready?" I asked.

"I don't know if I can handle another contraction," she said.

"Give me half of the pain," I said.

"I'll give you all of it if you want it," she said.

We shared a slight laugh that gave way to the contraction that brought Steven Leo Anderson into the world.

"Here comes the head," Dr. Hewitt said.

"Can you see it?" Claire screamed.

"Yeah, I can!" I shouted.

I could hardly see through my tear-stained eyes. My knees were wobbling, and the room spun in a dizzying circle.

"Here comes the baby!" Hewitt yelled.

I squeezed Claire's hand, as she surged forward and screamed.

"Oh my God," I cried. "I can see the head."

Hewitt worked the baby out of Claire and into the real world.

"You have a baby boy," Hewitt said.

"Is he all right?" Claire said. "Is everything where it's supposed to be?"

"He's perfectly healthy," Hewitt said.

They were working so quickly that I hardly followed what was going on. Claire's fingernails released my arm. They cleaned the baby, and Hewitt asked me if I wanted to cut the cord.

"I shouldn't," I said. Then I thought of Steven and the promise that I made to him. I took the scissors from Hewitt, and with shaking hands, I snipped the cord.

"Welcome, little boy," I said.

Hewitt handed the baby to me. I held everything that was right about the world in my arms. He was a golden sunrise. He was a crying, screaming gift from God. I brought him to Claire, and together we cried.

"Can we take him to Steven?" I asked.

The look on Hewitt's face told the complete story. Instantly I knew. Steven hadn't made it through.

Chapter Twenty-Three

– Coming of Age...Finally –

"The advantage of the emotions is that they lead us astray."
— *Oscar Wilde*

I don't know why, but the fact that Corey Magorey was signing autographs in the hospital lobby made me want to vomit. I didn't blame Corey as much as I blamed those who surrounded him. Yet, when he saw me, he broke away from the pack and pulled me into a bear hug.

"How are you?" he asked.

There were tears on his dark cheeks.

"I'm hanging," I said. "What're you doing here?"

"I got some time before the rookie game in Oakland. I wanted to make sure you were doing okay."

I had no idea how he might have found out about Steven's death.

"Amy called," he said, as though reading my mind.

"It's been rough," I said.

We moved through the building towards the grieving room. The hospital staff couldn't have been any more sympathetic. In the years to come, I would think back on their compassion with a heart filled with gratitude.

"How's Claire?" Corey asked.

"She's asleep," I said. "We took the baby down to Steven, but it wasn't how we imagined it."

"Life hardly ever works out," Corey said.

"She cried so hard. Her heart is just shattered. I never want to go through something like this again."

We were just a few steps from the room. Corey draped his arm around my shoulder and stopped me from entering.

"Like I've been trying to tell you. The pain you feel is because of how much you love these people. You know what's worse than losing love?"

I shrugged my shoulders.

"Never having it," Corey said. "That's the worse pain you can imagine."

At that moment, I realized how much I meant to him, and he to me.

"You know," he said, "I would've burned every last one of them dollars to keep Steven alive for you."

"I know," I said.

We hugged again.

"I need a new best friend," I said.

"Through thick and thin," he answered.

◊ ◊ ◊

Steven had pre-arranged his memorial service, and that was heart-breaking. I couldn't imagine sitting down and scripting out how the world would meet to say goodbye. Yet, he didn't want Claire to have to worry about it.

His body was cremated, and the memorial service was actually a church mass, with one person saying a few words about Steven's life. I had-n't truly expected it, but Steven bestowed me with the honor.

The church was hot and stuffy. I spent most of the mass concentrating on what I wanted to say, and how uncomfortable the tie was making me. I sat with Claire on one side, and Amy and Corey on the other. It seemed like one of us was always breaking down. Amy would cry for a while and then work to regain her composure. When she was done, Claire would lose it. I honestly didn't know which one to hug.

"At this point, Claire and Steven requested that Leo Brown say a few words," Father Peter Vickery said.

I started to stumble out of the seat, and Claire pulled my shoulder down enough to kiss me on the right cheek.

"You'll do fine," she whispered.

It was only about ten steps to the lectern, but when I arrived, I felt as though I had walked for three days.

179

"Steven had a wonderful life," I said.

I cleared my throat and paused for a moment. Just that one sentence had nearly finished me.

"He wanted me to tell everyone thank you. He wanted me to let you know that all of you made it wonderful."

Claire dabbed her eyes with a tissue. For a moment, it was almost as though we were suddenly alone together in the church.

"You can measure life any way you want, but in the end, it's all about how well you've loved, and how incredible it is to be loved. Steven loved everyone here, and he received more love in a short time...."

I didn't actually finish the sentence.

"I don't know how many lessons Steven actually taught me. We were just four years old when we met. We traded baseball cards, rode bikes, and played dodge ball. In the end, we couldn't actually dodge life."

Steven's mother emitted a loud sob that carried through the church. Soon enough, there were more people crying than not.

"I don't know the answer to get over the hurt we all feel. We were cheated out of more time with Steven. We're hurting because we can't understand how we'll be able to move on without him in our life."

I looked Amy squarely in the eyes.

"I understand that Steven would want you to learn a simple lesson: Make the most of your time. Love with all of your heart, and don't take life for granted. In the end, when someone is standing up here, talking about you, the finest thing that person might say is that you loved with your whole heart."

Once again, I paused so I might gain the strength to speak the final sentence.

"Steven had a wonderful life."

Under normal circumstances, I might have fallen from the altar, but I stepped away from the lectern and made my way back to my seat. Of course, Claire hugged me, but my speech had made me consider how I had treated Amy. When Claire let me go, I reached across her and pulled Amy into a bear hug. She softly cried on my shoulder.

"I'm so sorry," I whispered.

After the service, we gathered at Margaret's house. I'm not sure how to put it, but it seemed as if Margaret was grateful for the chance to accommodate us. If only my father could see me now.

I assembled a plate of food that I didn't actually want. One by one, everyone there congratulated me for doing such a wonderful job on the eulogy. I could have lived without the accolades. I took a seat beside Corey.

"So when does your plane leave?" I asked.

"Eight-thirty," he said. "You're coming out, right?"

"I planned on staying a few more days, but Claire wouldn't hear of it," I said. "Besides, how could I miss your first professional game?"

He wrapped his hands around a roast beef sandwich. I was amazed by the size of his hands, and the bite he took out of the sandwich.

"I think you're almost cured," he said.

Actually, I wasn't really sure what he said, as he talked right through his chewing.

"What?"

"You're cured," he said. "I think you're a man now."

I wasn't exactly sure what he meant. I thought of my father's words during that argument so long ago. He had chided me about becoming a man, and Corey was confirming it for me. I didn't get the chance to pursue it. A tall, slender girl stepped in front of me, holding little Steven.

"Hi, Leo," she said.

"Hi," I said, but I didn't have a clue as to who she was. Without even looking at Corey, I knew that this beauty had captured his attention. "Do I know you?"

"I'm Stephanie," she said.

My mind flashed me the image of the fat girl from high school. I thought back to how my brother had filled my pockets with dog biscuits.

"Yeah, I'm the girl who ate the dog biscuits," she said.

We both started to laugh, and suddenly, I remembered the conversation we had as our date came to an end. We had been feeling sorry for ourselves. I had wished that I was with Claire, and she had wanted to be with Steven. My mind carried me back to the exact words she had spoken.

The thing is, some day those looks will go away. Or maybe, your skin will clear up and I'll lose weight and get rid of these freaking glasses.

"Maybe the sky will fall, too," I said.

181

We both laughed. Stephanie held the dog biscuit up to her nose.

"Some day we'll all be even. Maybe I'll even be happier than Claire, who knows?"

She held the biscuit to her lips and I watched in horror as she took a bite.

"Why do dogs love these fucking things so much?" she asked.

She must have assumed that I had lost my mind. She was calling my name, but I didn't hear her. It was Corey's nudge that brought me back to reality.

"That was a wonderful eulogy," she said.

The baby was asleep in her arms. I leaned in and kissed him on the cheek.

"My favorite part is when you said, 'Make the most of your time. Love with all of your heart, and don't take life for granted.'"

I didn't know what I was going to do, but the world seemed to be spinning much too fast. Her words were driving me crazy.

"Stephanie, you look wonderful," I said. "I hope all your wishes come true. Please excuse me, though, I have some business to take care of."

Corey started to ask me something, but I couldn't hear him, either.

◊ ◊ ◊

I found her a few minutes later. She was sitting on the outside step with a plate of food in her lap. Her head was down, and she hadn't seen my approach, but her new boyfriend had.

"Hey, Leo," he said. "Honey, wasn't Leo's eulogy wonderful?"

Amy looked deep into my eyes. I knew she could see straight into my heart.

"Thanks, Keith," I said.

I hadn't even looked at him.

"It's Ken," he said.

"Yeah, all right. Can I talk to Amy alone?"

He started to voice a protest, but Amy cut him off. Slowly, he gathered his plate and shuffled away.

"I was talking about you today," I said. "I can't believe I let you walk away."

"You didn't 'let' me do anything," she said.

"You know what I mean," I said.

She stabbed a forkful of macaroni salad.

"Leo, you're just emotional. I'm with Kevin now."

"It's Ken, isn't it?"

She continued eating. If I didn't know better, I would have thought she was actually enjoying the moment.

"Yes, it's Ken," she said. "I don't want to get in a serious discussion about life right now. I was trying to be funny."

She batted her eyelashes, and I forced a smile. I felt the sweat beading up on the back of my neck. I yanked at my tie.

"The thing is, I'm leaving for California tomorrow, and I want you to go with me. We can work our way through this."

Amy set the plate of food on the step beside her. She opened her arms and I hugged her for all that I was worth.

"I'm with Ken," she said. "I can't just leave him."

I didn't want the embrace to end, but she pulled away.

"Do you love him?" I asked.

She turned to look at him. He stood at the end of the driveway, kicking rocks into the ditch. He was trying not to look at us.

"Leo, I don't have to answer that," she said.

So, my final stand had been met and handily defeated. I pulled her into a hug, and she cried into my ear.

"Have fun in California," she whispered. "Try to catch your breath a little bit."

I wanted to explain that I was seeing it all so clearly now. I had finally come to grips with my feelings for Claire. I understood I had wasted too much time. Amy had been the girl that was really there, and I had taken her for granted.

"I love you," I said.

If she heard me, she didn't let on. Ken, or Kevin, or Keith, or whoever the hell it was, made his way back to her side. If this was the first day of my real life, it wasn't what I expected.

Chapter Twenty-Four

– Now what? –

"I was going to buy a book on positive thinking and then I thought 'what the hell good would that do?'"
— *Woody Allen*

It all hit me as I settled into my seat on the flight from Oakland to Boston. In the past couple of weeks, I had given the eulogy at my best friend's funeral, watched the love of my life give birth to another man's child, visited my mother in California where I watched the youngest, richest, professional athlete, who happened to be my new best friend, score fourteen points in his Celtics debut. Oh yeah, I had also officially lost my girlfriend of better than three years. It all read like a bad novel.

I laid my seat back, but the flight attendant reminded me to sit upright. When I closed my eyes, I saw my mother's face. The California sun was good to her. She didn't look as if she had aged a day since she left Buffalo. Her words rang in my ears, and I could almost feel her embrace.

"I'm so proud of you. You've become a good man."

Above all else, maybe she was right. Perhaps all we can hope for in life is to appreciate that our children have grown up to be decent, productive people. It had been her life's work, and while I missed her, I couldn't begrudge her the life she built with Keith. I wondered if she missed my father, and I'm sure there were days when she truly did. Life seemed to be all about living and loving, and making mistakes and then correcting them. Maybe they had made a mistake, but if they hadn't been together, I wouldn't have even existed. Looking back, they still had to be proud of what they'd created together.

The plane moved down the runway. The first rush of speed brought me forward in my seat, and I watched the pavement speed by me. Everything in my life had happened so fast, but I felt as though it had unfolded in slow motion. The stranglehold of my love for Claire had mercifully slipped away. Somehow, things had changed. While I loved her even more, it was a different sort of love. I had heard that love was just a state of mind. Watching Claire give birth put a different spin on all of it. It felt strange not to be *in love* with her.

I had a long layover in Chicago, and I stumbled through the massive airport terminal. It was the middle of the afternoon, and the place was a bustle of activity. I arrived in the general proximity of my gate and sat in a hard, red chair. I had a book to read and a column to write, but I just wanted to sit there.

I felt as though a veil had been lifted from my eyes. In the hurried glance of each passing face, I saw evidence of life, and the price we pay to live it to the fullest. I was reminded of sitting with Steven as he explained that the prospect of death had provided him clarity. We all have a story to tell and an unknown time to tell it. I could only wonder what the anonymous people thought of me as I buried my head in my hands and sobbed. I cried for Steven in death, and myself in life. All that I desired was to be thought of as a good man.

◊ ◊ ◊

Three months later, I received a call from Claire. While we routinely spoke a couple of times a week, this call seemed a bit different.

"Will you be Steven's Godfather?" she asked.

"Of course."

So, I was aboard another Buffalo-bound airplane. My life had ironed out a bit. I was a twenty-six-year-old man with a high-paying job. As a bachelor that couldn't get a date, I was able to save quite a bit of money. Yet, I was horribly lonely.

Claire and little Steven picked me up at the airport. We chatted about Corey's exciting life as a professional athlete, and the lives we had settled into. As she pulled out into traffic with the baby secured in the backseat, I considered her appearance. She looked every bit as amazing as she always had. She had quickly dropped the pregnancy weight.

"You look awesome," I said.

She smiled a bit, and nodded in the direction of the backseat.

"Sleep depravation is a miserable thing. He's up every three hours, and unfortunately, I can't just nudge Steven and tell him to go get the baby."

"How *are* you?" I asked.

"I'm good." She smiled nervously and glanced at me. "Late at night it really gets to me, but Steven's still around, you know?"

"He always will be."

"The thing is, I want it to hurt because if it stops hurting, it'll be like I'm forgetting him. Do you know what I mean? Isn't that strange?"

Yet, it wasn't strange at all.

"Hey, you know what I was thinking?" she asked.

"What's that?"

"I was thinking you should make me dinner."

"Oh, you were, huh?"

She laughed so sweetly that my heart jumped in my chest in that old familiar way.

"Little Steven and I will take our naps, and you can serve me like the queen that I am."

"I can do that," I said.

There wasn't anything else I would've rather done.

Three hours later, I stood over a pot of boiling water. I was preparing fettuccine alfredo and chicken breasts sautéed in a garlic and mushroom sauce, and topped with mozzarella cheese. I cleaned the dishes as I cooked, so all there was left to do was watch the water boil.

From my spot in the kitchen, I saw clear into the living room. Claire held Steven in her lap and the chair rocked back and forth. I always knew she'd make a wonderful mother. I heard Claire's voice over the sound of the boiling water as she softly sang to her baby. I closed my eyes and imagined their life together. Although Steven would never know his father, something told me they'd be all right. Somehow, Claire would make it work.

Steven slept peacefully through dinner. I didn't know much about babies, but he seemed to be fairly low maintenance. Claire and I shared a bottle of wine over dinner, talking about Steven, Corey, my mother, and finally, my last conversation with Amy.

"Dinner was awesome," she said. "You can cook for me anytime."

I nearly offered to make her dinner every night for the rest of her life, but again, I just didn't see myself in her future.

"Life goes so fast," she said. "I remember the day we met."

"What were we, about four?" I asked.

"Yeah, we were playing street hockey, and your brother was picking on you."

"You stuck up for me, right?"

"Always," she said. "I told Michael that I'd bloody his nose if he didn't stop teasing you."

There was a bit of an awkward silence as we drifted back in time.

"Why'd you become my guardian?" I asked.

She leaned back in the chair and flicked her hair with a flip of the hand. She smiled mischievously and sipped her wine.

"Because you needed one. Don't take this wrong, but you still do."

"Was I that pathetic? Am I still pathetic?"

She glanced at the baby in the far corner of the room.

"Steven and I used to talk about it. He always said that I'd be a good mother because I spent so much time taking care of you."

"That's about it," I said. "I probably wouldn't have made it if you weren't there."

I poured the last of the wine into our glasses. Claire got up and walked over to the baby's bassinet. She was wearing a pair of jean shorts and a bright red blouse. I watched her every step of the way, just as I always had.

"My baby is so peaceful, but there's so much to worry about."

She leaned over the bassinet. She adjusted his blanket and kissed him.

"I wonder if he'll be like Steven. It drives me crazy with worry when I think about the bad things he'll have to face."

She returned to the table, pulled her chair close, and grabbed my hand. She held it so tenderly that my heart jumped into my throat.

"He's so innocent, but no matter what I do, he's going to have to struggle to understand life."

Claire was whispering. She traced a path along the palm of my hand.

"You were always the same way. You were innocent and naïve, and it seemed like real life was going to eventually break your heart."

She set the wine glass down and leaned even closer. She was just inches from me.

"We were always so worried about hurting you. When Steven realized he was dying, he constantly talked about how perfect it would be if you and I ended up together. Sometimes I think he was more worried about you than me."

I don't know what made me do it, but I tilted her head back and kissed her lips. She didn't resist and I pulled her up from the chair and onto my lap. We kissed one another hungrily. I concentrated on the feel of her lips on mine. I had imagined it so many times that she actually felt familiar in my arms.

"I love you."

She whispered the words so quietly that I wondered if I'd actually heard them.

"I love you too," I said.

She kissed me again, but gently pulled away from me.

"You do realize we *aren't* going to end up together," she said.

The baby stirred awake with a cry. The kiss, and the abrupt ending to all of it, confused me.

"In reality, my heart belongs to Steven," she said. She touched the side of my face. "As for you, I know that if you think hard enough, you'll understand where your heart truly belongs."

She kissed me as though she were kissing me goodbye.

"I always told Steven we'd be around to take care of each other."

"We will," I whispered.

"It was a great kiss, but if I'm going to take care of you, I've got to do it right."

The baby shrieked as though it had been his job to signal an end to the romantic moment. Claire tended to him as I sat back wondering what the hell had just happened. In the years to follow, I would remember it simply as an expression of our love.

◊ ◊ ◊

I stood beside Claire at the front of the church as Father Vickery explained the ceremony and the importance of baptism. Claire held the sleeping child, and I couldn't take my eyes off the two of them.

"So, I see the Godfather, and the baby, of course. Do we have a Godmother?"

"I'm here."

The voice came from the back of the church. When I turned to see whom it belonged to, the sunshine blocked my vision. Amy stepped out of the sunshine, and I turned to Claire.

"Amy?" I asked.

I felt a little queasy in the stomach and shaky in the knees. It was exactly how I felt as a child when Claire would walk by.

"We've talked every day," Claire whispered.

I couldn't help but smile.

"Why, of course you have," I said.

"I promised to take care of you," Claire said. She was smiling smugly. Amy was on her way up the aisle. Once again, she was late. She looked hurried, disorganized, and undeniably wonderful.

"That's who you belong with," Claire whispered. "If she gives you another chance, you'd better not blow it."

189

Chapter Twenty-Five

– Resolution –

"Everything has been figured out except how to live."
— *Jean Paul Sartre*

It was a curious alignment to say the least. Claire and Amy were on either side of me and baby Steven was in my arms. The child didn't have any idea what was happening, but his tiny finger gripped my index finger as Father Vickery addressed us.

"Holy Baptism is basically the first sacrament. It's the door to the spiritual life, and is essentially Steven Leo's introduction to the real world."

I couldn't help but imagine that I was also receiving a dose of life. I stole a glance at the two wonderful women beside me. Claire smiled as tears threatened her eyes, and Amy's smile was one of wonderment and surprise.

"You know, Baptism means a lot of things to a lot of different people. Some people stand before me without even the semblance of an idea of what it all means. Others make the commitment out of love, and still others do it out of fear."

Father Vickery seemed to be talking directly to me. He cleared his throat and continued in a silky tone.

"Like any of the sacraments, you must be willing to give with your whole heart. In respect to life itself, I'm sure that you all understand that it works best when you're able to extend trust, hope, faith, and love as a whole package."

Steven emitted a soft cry, and all eyes turned to him.

"You know what I'm talking about, right, Steven?"

There was a bit of laughter from those gathered behind me.

"Of course, Steven doesn't have a clue as to why he's here, or why we'll be touching his forehead with water. That's why you're all here. Leo and Amy have very important jobs in regard to the direction of Steven's spiritual life. Leo, can you tell me why we're baptizing Steven?"

"It's for the remission of sin, isn't it?" I said.

Amy smiled as though she were proud of me.

"He's basically paying for the sins of the past," I said.

I never took my eyes from Amy.

"It's a rebirth and a redirection, and it's a ceremony to wipe the slate clean, so to speak."

Father Vickery took a step back and placed his hand over his heart.

"That's the best answer I ever got to that question. Steven is blessed to be entering life surrounded by this group."

There really wasn't anything I could do to stop the tears. As Father Vickery held Steven to the water, I thought of the cycle of life. I considered my father's death and my life. I contemplated Steven's death and the arrival of his son.

I extended my hand to Amy, and she took it, offering a tight squeeze and tears of her own.

"I baptize thee in the name of the Father and of the Son and of the Holy Spirit."

As we left the church, I felt as though I were born anew. I felt Claire's eyes upon me, and when I turned to her, she looked down to where my hand was coupled with Amy. She smiled, and mouthed the words, *I'm proud of you.*

It occurred to me that she was simply the guardian angel of my life.

It was early evening, and we walked along Long Island Shore. It was nearly fall, but summer hadn't yet threatened to leave. The disappearing sun still shone down brightly. We held hands, knowing that we'd received our second chance.

"If you love something set it free," Amy said.

"I always thought that was ridiculous," I said.

191

Clifford Fazzolari

"It worked here, didn't it?"

We moved down the pier and settled in at the edge of the dock. The water was still and clear as glass.

"So, what happened to Kevin?" I asked.

"It was Ken, wasn't it?" Amy asked.

I turned her face with a gentle touch of my hand and we kissed.

"He was a good guy," she said, "but I never really stopped thinking about you. He'll be all right. Actually, I did a lot of thinking while we were apart. I learned to take life for what it is, and not to try and read too much into it. I guess I appreciate the little things a lot more."

"That's quite a coincidence," I said, "because that's what I learned, too."

We kissed once more, but in the back of my mind there was a sliver of doubt.

"Why'd you come back? I really wasn't good to you."

"Let's just say that a little bird was whispering in my ear."

"Claire?"

"Who else? She kept me updated on your personal growth. She has so much faith in you, and she knows you so well."

A couple of seagulls passed by. In the background, the sinking sun was bright orange.

"This is like a perfect moment, isn't it?" Amy whispered.

Truer words had never been spoken. Our lips met in a long kiss. We broke our embrace, and I helped Amy to her feet.

"Actually, there's one thing that's bothering me a little," I said.

There was fear in her eyes. I wrapped my arms around her and laughed.

"It's nothing like that," I said.

"What is it?"

The debate raged in my mind, but I knew I had to do it.

"Remember when you thought you were pregnant?"

She instantly knew what was about to happen, but I didn't let her break away. As deftly as I could, I tossed her off the dock and into the water below.

I stood above her as she coughed and laughed her way back through the surface of the water. She didn't know it, but I was crying. I jumped into the water beside her, and she leaped onto my back, and tried to force my

192

head under the water. For the first time in my life, everything seemed crystal clear to me.

Corey Magorey was the leading candidate for the rookie-of-the-year award, and the season was only fourteen games old. As was our habit, we met at center court precisely twenty minutes before tip-off. It was a tribute to our finest moment together just after the NCAA championship. We shook hands as though we hadn't seen one another in weeks.

"Are they here yet?" Corey asked.

The Fleet Center was filled to half-capacity.

"Are you kidding me?" I asked. "Claire wanted to come down here at noon."

"We got the Lakers tonight," Corey said. "Man, Shaq is a bitch."

"Just relax," I said. "This isn't brain surgery, right?"

Corey laughed as though it were the first time I had ever said the words. Truth be told, our pre-game chat rarely varied from night to night.

"Everything's set," Corey said.

"Yeah, I know," I said.

"I better get back," he said.

We shook hands once more. Just as he did every night, he bent down to my left ear.

"We make our own reality," he whispered. "Love and lose, love and win, dust yourself off and love again."

We were seated directly behind the Celtics bench. Claire and Amy talked non-stop about everything from the color of little Steven's shit to the way Kobe Bryant's ass looked in his shorts.

"Incredible," I said.

"No, really," Claire said, "back in the eighties, they used to wear short little shorts that rode up their ass. Now everyone's shorts are so baggy that you can't even make out their shape."

Corey was on fire. He made his first seven shots from the field, and twice he went directly at Shaquille O'Neal. Yet, I was having a difficult time concentrating on the game. I just wanted halftime to hurry up and arrive. I sipped a beer and tried to imagine how it would all work out.

"Hey, dream boy," Claire waved her hand in front of my eyes. "I'm going to get some nachos, you want anything?"

"No, I'm perfect," I said.

Claire glared at me, and I knew what she was thinking. I had to act natural or I would blow it. I moved into Claire's seat beside Amy.

"Hey, love chunks," she said.

I kissed her, but she pushed me away.

"It's a one point game," she said.

Corey stole the ball and raced down the sidelines directly in front of us. His two-handed jam brought the crowd to its feet and gave the Celtics the lead.

"He's awesome," Amy screamed.

I watched the clock tick away the last few seconds of the half. Claire came down the aisle with the nachos. She winked at me, and I smiled.

"I'm starving," Amy said. "Whose idea was it to have dinner after the game?"

The horn sounded to end the half. I stayed in the seat beside Amy, and Claire nestled in behind me. Amy took a tortilla chip and dipped it into the cheese. Somehow, she missed the ring completely.

"Hey, change seats with Claire," Amy said. "I want to sit next to her."

"Isn't that nice," I said.

She reached across me, and dipped another chip into the cheese. This time, she got the ring.

"What the hell is this?" she said.

She wiped the cheese away and screamed.

"Will you marry me?" I asked.

She threw her arms around my shoulders, and I felt nacho cheese on the back of my neck. The scoreboard flashed my question, and I pointed to it.

"Of course!" she screamed.

After a moment, we considered Claire.

"Well, Leo, my boy, I guess you found that love you were looking for," Claire said.

We pulled her into our circle. I took the envelope from my back pocket.

"I have something for you too," I said. "This is for Steven's college fund, or whatever."

Claire opened the envelope, and peered at the two checks.

"You're giving him twenty-five grand?"

"Yeah, and the other one's from Corey."

Claire simply lost it. She buried her head in her hands.

"I didn't want your money. I only asked for your love and friendship."

It was hard to tell if she was happy or sad. Amy quickly solved the problem.

"Take the cash," she whispered.

$$\Diamond \quad \Diamond \quad \Diamond$$

We stood out on the sidewalk in front of the Fleet Center. The enthusiasm of the fans was contagious, and everyone that passed by thanked their lucky stars for Corey Magorey.

"People are just looking for something to hang their hats on," Claire said. "Everyone wants to be entertained and happy. That isn't too much to ask?"

"Don't start talking in riddles again," I said.

She pulled me into a hug. Amy cleared her throat from behind us.

"Oh, lovebirds, this is Leo's fiancée announcing that I'm going to the bathroom before we leave," Amy said.

I kissed her, but still held Claire close as Amy disappeared into the crowd.

"I promised Steven that I'd take care of you," I said.

"Yeah, right," Claire said. "I promised him that I'd take care of *you*."

We laughed and kissed as a mother might kiss a child.

"I'll be fine," she said.

"I know you will."

The limousine pulled up to the curb.

"There's our ride," I said.

195

It was a long, white stretch limo with tinted back windows. If I knew Corey, it was filled with champagne, food, and loud music.

"You are the greatest," I said.

Claire flashed her lovely smiled and bowed her head.

"Promise me that you'll love Amy even more," she said.

I pulled her into another hug, and we held the embrace for a moment.

"Geez, look at this," Amy yelled. "They're still freaking hugging."

The driver arrived on the scene as I struggled to gain my composure.

"Can I assist you into the car?" he asked.

The driver was in a tuxedo, complete with a top hat. He extended his hand to Claire.

"It's like a fairytale," I said.

"There he goes again," Claire said. "Leo still thinks there's a Santa Claus."

We drank champagne, ate caviar, and were escorted through downtown Boston in a long stretch limo.

"I wish Weird Henry could see us now," I said.

"He can," Claire said.

She raised her glass in a toast.

"He's watching with Steven and your Dad. They're saying, 'look at them lucky son-of-a-bitches.'"

We clanked glasses and toasted life. Real life.